HOW TO SURVIVE AN UNDEAD HONEYMOON

HAILEY EDWARDS

HOW TO SURVIVE AN UNDEAD HONEYMOON

The Epilogues: Part II

Nothing says romance like spending a long weekend at a haunted inn famed for sending its guests to the ER with scratches, bites, and fractures. Or so Linus thinks when he books a trip for Grier and himself to Oliphant House. As far as honeymoons go, the choice is nontraditional, but then, so is his bride.

Haunted history is one of Grier's great loves, and she's thrilled to discover Linus has given her a mystery to solve. Forget walks on moonlit beaches and sipping fruity drinks, Grier would much rather unravel the curse that's plagued the Oliphant family for generations than pick sand from between her toes.

The resident spooks, however, aren't happy with the newlyweds sticking their noses where they don't belong. Between the missing persons, the dead bodies, and the secrets lurking in the basement, Linus and Grier start to wonder if they'll survive their honeymoon.

MAKE NO APOLOGIES
for surviving

ONE

"Mr. and Mrs. Woolworth," an elderly man warbled at us with a dentured smile. "Our honeymooners."

Linus never failed to surprise me, and his choice of post-wedding destination did not disappoint.

The cozy bed-and-breakfast smack-dab in the middle of nowhere Delaware was adorable. I could picture us cuddling in bed, reading in bed, eating in bed, and other activities best suffixed with *in bed*. But what I couldn't imagine was how Linus had selected this pinprick on a map for our quickie romantic getaway.

Curiosity sharpened my gaze while I searched for what, exactly, about the remote inn had intrigued him.

"We've been expecting you," the man continued, wiry glasses slipping down his bulbous nose before catching on the wide flare of his nostrils. "I'm so pleased you chose us to take these first steps with you as man and wife."

About to thank him for his hospitality, I opened my mouth and coughed when brimstone hit the back of my throat. The potent fragrance of dark magic rolled over my skin a moment later, and I shivered, easing closer to Linus.

"The inn is lovely." He wrapped a proprietary arm around my waist. "We're looking forward to our stay."

The old man preened at the compliment and adjusted his glasses with a practiced nudge from his pinky.

"Kyle will show you to your room." Mr. Oliphant rang a bell behind the counter, and a teen sporting a faux hawk braided tight against his skull emerged with a scowl pulling at his bottom lip piercing. Dressed head to toe in more shades of pink than a flamingo, I envied that flare for color coordination. I couldn't have gotten it right without help from Neely. "Escort the Woolworths to their room."

"It's *Kylie*, Gramps." He—no, *she*—crossed her arms over her chest. "We talked about this."

"I had a Kyle for sixteen years." He waved a gnarled hand. "Give me longer than a week to get used to having a Kylie." He snapped his fingers then pointed one at her. "I'll remember next time."

"Sure, you will." She snorted. "And Grams will remember where she put her reading glasses the next time she loses them." Tall and lean, Kylie vaulted over the counter with the ease of someone who had performed the move a million times and landed in front of Linus. "Where are your bags?"

"In the car." Linus held up a key fob Kylie was quick to snatch. "In the trunk."

Kylie grumbled under her breath about having better things to do and heaved a put-upon sigh.

The cool stare Linus gave her, what I thought of as his Scion Lawson mask, put starch in the kid's spine.

Southern manners being ingrained in Georgia girls from birth, I almost stepped into the breach to smooth things over when it hit me.

That wasn't his Scion Lawson mask.

It was his Scion *Woolworth* mask now.

Giddiness bubbled up in me, and I couldn't stop my smile from spreading until my cheeks hurt. Mr. Oliphant answered my grin with one of his own as he palmed the key to our room.

"You're welcome to go on up," he said with a conspiratorial wink.

"I would take you, but my knees aren't what they used to be. Stairs are for the young."

"That would be great." I accepted the key, which was attached to a thin wooden disc with a hand-carved room number. "We're tired after our flight. I wouldn't mind grabbing a nap before dinner."

And I wouldn't mind stealing a word with *Mr.* Woolworth about our accommodations.

Mr. Woolworth.

Heh.

That silly thrill returned, swelling my heart until it had trouble fitting in my chest.

Linus shot me a questioning glance, but I kept my head down to minimize how ridiculous I felt basking in the glow of overwhelming happiness whenever I thought of him as *mine*. With the rings to prove it.

We hit the wide staircase together, and the sense of wrongness increased as we climbed higher. The magic was...odd. Brittle and sharp. Jagged edges that scraped along my senses. And phew boy. It was check-the-bottom-of-your-shoes foul.

Our suite resembled my bedroom back at Woolworth House, with its polished oak floors and handmade quilts piled high on the queen mattress. Once inside, I used the pocketknife I had stolen from Linus forever ago to prick my finger and draw a sigil on the doorframe to seal us in.

Turning to face him, I cocked an eyebrow, ready to hear this. "You have interesting ideas about romantic getaways."

The ring on his finger had inspired new confidence in him, and he backed me against the door, pinning my hips there with his. "I had limited options."

Mm-hmm.

More like *un*limited options.

Unable to resist touching him, I traced the faint twitch in his cool lips. "How did you say that with a straight face?"

"I've been practicing," he confessed. "I wanted to get this right."

"You worry too much." I tapped his chin. "You have yet to disappoint me." I winked just to watch heat warm his cheeks. "In any way."

"Money makes you anxious." He trailed chilly fingers along my collarbone. "You don't like to spend it, and you're uncomfortable when I do. That eliminated our more exotic options."

There was nothing I could say to that except, "Go on."

"One of your great passions is haunted history," he said with the authority of a man who had purchased an entire building for me so that I could start my own ghost tour company. "Oliphant House was built in 1665 and converted into a boarding house after the owner's death. It served as one of the earliest inns in the northeast. It has an interesting history and a thoroughly documented haunting. Those two things led me to believe this location might be the ideal combination of thrift and amusement."

"You know me so well." I melted into the teasing caress of his fingertips. "Do go on."

The touching and the talking, in no particular order.

"Chandler Oliphant built his home over an energy nexus, what he called in his journals a gateway to biblical Hell. He meant its design to trap any evil spirits or demons who might emerge in a subterranean maze of halls that lead nowhere, windows painted shut, and doors that open onto sealed walls."

"Okay." I hooked my fingers in his belt loops. "You officially have my attention."

In more ways than one.

"He lived here the rest of his life and raised a family without seeing a single beast or hearing even one inexplicable noise. He went to his grave content that he had done his Christian duty and that whatever great evil lurked beneath his home was trapped within his construct. Or so the story goes."

Tugging on the back of his shirt, I untucked it from his pants. "Well that's disappointing."

"However, on the thirtieth anniversary of Chandler Oliphant's death," he continued, a slight hitch in his breath when I skimmed his spine, "several guests were attacked by unseen forces." Black flickered in his eyes, darkening the navy hue. "Victims reported scratches that might have come from—"

"A demon in desperate need of a manicure?"

"How did you guess?" The corners of his eyes crinkled. "Since then, every thirty years to the day, at least one guest per cycle is harmed by *The Hell Demon of Oliphant House.*"

"I heard those italics, mister." Fingers gone still, I gazed up at him. "Does it make me a bad person that I'm interested again?"

"Not even a little bit." He kissed the tip of my nose. "Would you like to hear the rest?"

"You missed your calling." I unbuttoned the shirt then smoothed my hands across his chest, all lean muscle and glimmering ink, his skin pebbling under my fingers. "You should be a guide for my ghost tours."

"There's another reason why I thought this place's history might appeal to you."

"Let me guess." I pushed the shirt off his shoulders. "This week is the anniversary?"

"Yes."

"I was joking." Eyes widening, I gaped up at him. "Are you serious?"

"This was the trip I had in mind when I asked that the wedding date be shifted accordingly, yes."

"Wow." I forgot what I was doing for a minute. "Are we the only guests?"

"Yes." The hint of smugness looked good on him. "I booked the entire inn for our stay."

"You get that if we're the only guests, we're the only targets, right?"

He slid his hands behind me and stroked my skin in cool sweeps of his thumbs. "That was the idea."

"You booked us into a violently haunted house on the anniversary of its founder's death to be one half of a pair of sacrificial lambs," I said in summation. "For our honeymoon."

A beat of hesitation, a crinkle of his brow, gave away his worry. "Yes?"

"You really know how to show a girl a good time." I linked my arms around his neck. "How did I get so lucky?"

"I can't tell if you're teasing me," he admitted, searching my face for clues. "Did I disappoint you?"

"This is nothing I could have imagined," I confessed. "It's so much *better*." I grinned at him. "Mystery. Food. Mauling." The drive in from the airport had given us a short tour of the nearest town, and its total lack of takeout, dining, and entertainment options. "There is food, right?"

"Yes." He leaned down, his breath fanning my cheeks. "I had groceries delivered yesterday."

"You're going to cook for me?" I raked my fingers through his dark-auburn hair. "Are you sure? This is your honeymoon too. I don't want you to work so hard you can't enjoy it."

"I have plenty of time for it that won't interfere with our activities."

The few hours Linus slept each week left him with twice as much time on his hands as the rest of us. Lately, he dozed off and on if he stayed in bed with me, but he required little REM to function.

"All right." I rose on tiptoe and kissed my favorite smattering of freckles, the daisy-shaped cluster beneath his left eye. "But let me know if you change your mind."

"There's the added benefit of allowing Mrs. Oliphant to stay home."

She must be the cook to her husband's concierge, neither of which would be needed this week.

"Ah." I should have put it together sooner. "You're kicking the Oliphants out too."

Two less bodies in the house doubled our odds of getting attacked.

Yay?

"I have to admit, I'm surprised you chose this." I made a small hop, and Linus caught my legs around his waist. "You're usually opposed to me getting even the least bit maimed."

"You can take care of yourself." He carried me to the bed. "I can't imagine whatever is haunting this place is more dangerous than anything we've faced together so far."

Otherwise, it went without saying, he never would have brought me here.

I squealed when he tossed me onto the mattress then laughed when he landed on top of me in a press of now-familiar weight.

"You can tell me if you're disappointed." He brushed his fingers across my cheek, my nose, my lips. "I always thought I would take you to a remote island where I could have you all to myself." He softened his voice. "You used to love the beach."

More to the point, I had loved a woman who lived on the beach. Odette Lecomte, the next best thing I'd had to an aunt growing up, and the person who had betrayed my parents, Maud, and me.

Sand, surf, and sun no longer held any appeal. I hadn't visited Tybee Island in years. It held too many memories. I wasn't in a rush to walk any other beaches either. The roar of the waves, the tang in the air, the grains between my toes, would remind me of the good times and that they were all a lie.

"I always pictured a beachy honeymoon." There was no point in lying about it. He knew me too well for that. "But I can't see it anymore. That's why I was relieved when you offered to take over the planning. I had no idea what I wanted to do or where I wanted to go, and you've been everywhere at least once."

"I have traveled a lot." His work, both as a professor at Strophalos University and his private necromancy practice, plus his former position as Scion Lawson, had carried him all over the world. "That doesn't mean I explored those cities or did more than show up for lectures or perform resuscitations before retreating to my hotel room to read."

"How could you visit Rome or Greece or Ireland and not go out for gelato or spanakopita or colcannon?"

"I didn't eat then," he reminded me, "and the world had long since lost its flavor."

From what I gathered, Linus hadn't lived much during my imprisonment in Atramentous. He wouldn't call it a self-imposed punishment, but that's how I saw it. He had worked hard, made solid friends, and performed his duties as the Potentate of Atlanta to the best of his considerable abilities, but even the art he created during that period tended more toward black and gray.

"Lucky for you, you've got me." I linked my feet at his spine. "I'm willing to eat my way through Europe and anywhere else."

"I am lucky," he said, earnestness and puzzlement and happiness all rolled into his tone.

Three loud knocks on the door spared him from the sound pinching he deserved for finding himself even a teensy-tiny bit unworthy. It must be Kylie with our luggage.

Fiddlesticks.

I knew I should have searched for a *do not disturb* sign.

<h1 style="text-align:center">TWO</h1>

The disgruntled teen at the door looked about as thrilled to be standing there as I was to have to put on pants again. I noticed her noticing Linus's shirt wasn't buttoned up to his throat, and the few that had been fastened in his haste fit the wrong holes.

"Sorry to interrupt." She trudged into the room with our luggage rolling behind her. "You guys can get back to it in just a second." She left the bags and opened the closet. "I get docked if I don't do the whole shebang." She came out holding two mismatched wooden stands, flicked her wrists, and set up the luggage racks. "Do you want any of your stuff hung up, or is this good?"

With a grunt, she heaved each of our big suitcases onto their respective racks.

"That's good," I rushed to assure her. "We can handle it from here."

Our bags contained items hard to explain to humans, plus Neely had stuffed mine with lingerie I was too embarrassed to look at, let alone model for Linus. There were swimsuits in there too, which I wouldn't need, and a few fancy dresses with even fancier shoes that also wouldn't come in handy while sleuthing.

Linus opened his wallet, let her notice its fullness. "How long have you worked at the inn?"

"Officially?" Kylie tongued her piercing, flicking it back and forth. "About two years."

"Have you experienced anything strange during your time here?"

A knowing smile sharpened her eyes. "You're ghost hunters."

"Something like that," he agreed, pulling out a fifty-dollar bill, which he dispensed the way most of us handed out fives. "Well?" He passed it over. "Any paranormal phenomenon to report?"

Weighing her words against the heft of his wallet, she appeared to debate what we wanted to hear.

"Tell us the truth," I urged gently. "Trust me, he tips better when you're honest."

That gave her pause, but she came to a decision and closed the door behind her.

"There's a smell in the kitchen," she whispered as if her grandfather were standing in the hall. "I thought it was eggs gone bad, but Grams claims she doesn't notice it." She shrugged. "She's old, so maybe her nose doesn't work like it used to, but come on. It seriously reeks in there."

Haunted kitchen.

Check.

All those sharp knives were practically begging to stab someone. What violent ghost wouldn't set up camp in there?

"That's all?" Linus prompted, already selecting the next bill in his stack.

"I got shoved down the stairs once, but that was back when I was a kid." Kylie glowered. "Gramps didn't believe me." She held up her arm, flashing a deep scar across her elbow. "He blamed me, said I must have left a toy on the stairs."

Well, okay, so calling it a ghost had been polite. Obviously, we were dealing with a poltergeist...or worse.

Hand on Linus's sleeve, I kept him from forking over quite yet. "Can you think of any other incidents?"

"Guests report weird stuff all the time, but other than the stink and the shove, no."

Pungent *and* violent. The telltale thrill that always preceded the hunt kindled along my nerves. "When did the smell start?"

"Two days ago? Something like that?"

"Thank you." Linus passed her the bill once I released him. "We appreciate your candor."

"No problem." She crammed the money into her pocket. "Dial two if you need anything. It goes direct to my cell, so I'll get the call even from home." A tighter shrug twitched her shoulders. "We live in the cottage behind the property. It's not a long walk, and I'm up late most nights."

"We'll do that." Linus escorted her out then appraised me with a thoughtful tilt of his chin. "What do you think?"

"That you don't understand the value of a dollar, or that you have some bizarre affliction that makes you unable to read zeroes. Either of those would explain why you grease palms with such large bills when half that amount would do."

"People who are hesitant to cooperate often find themselves more willing to do so when the sum of money they stand to earn far exceeds their expectations."

Given he was the one who taught me the art of cultivating informants through bribery, I couldn't knock his system. Though, granted, I was still more likely to offer a twenty and reserve my fifties for the hard cases. Linus just preferred to go big and save time.

"You're lucky you were born filthy rich is all I'm saying."

"You're both richer and cheaper than I am."

"I can't decide if that last part is an insult, but I'll own it."

There was a time after Atramentous when I struggled to keep the lights on. Money was tight, food was a luxury item, and I spent a lot of time sitting in dark rooms to save on the power bill. Ketchup on crackers was not gourmet, let me tell you. Neither was dry ramen dusted with a flavor packet. After eating that a few times, I never forgot the cutoff date for the water again.

"How about frugal?" He crossed to me, resting his hands on my waist. "Better?"

"I can live with frugal." I decided not to tell him he could call me anything he wanted if his hands kept doing what they were doing. "It has a higher-end ring to it."

About to resume our newlywed activities, I growled in frustration when a dark figure wearing a tattered cloak with a shadowed cowl coalesced behind Linus.

"Cletus." I exhaled through my teeth. "We talked about this."

The wraith was never more than a summons away, but he groaned yet another throaty complaint about us gallivanting off alone. We had left him with Oscar and Keet at Lethe's house with strict orders not to follow, but he must have decided he knew best. A very Maud-like trait, if you asked me.

"Grier and I would appreciate some privacy." Linus tried his hand negotiating with him. "We'll call if anything happens."

If.

Often, it was a matter of *when*, but maybe this time the odds would be in our favor. A wedding gift from the universe. Wouldn't that be nice?

Sometimes being Grier Woolworth, Dame Woolworth, and the Potentate of Savannah all rolled into one made me tired. And then there was the mother-in-law factor. The Grande Dame wasn't the *call me Mom* kind. More like the *bow before me* type. Let's just say, despite being on decent terms with her, she and I weren't in danger of coordinating mother/daughter ensembles anytime soon.

Not that he would breathe one word of complaint, but Linus must feel the same way. His title and duties were as much a burden as mine. Just this once, we had wanted to jet off and go on an adventure for two. Backup was always smart, given the targets painted on our backs at any given moment, but I wanted Linus to myself for a change.

Still, I understood why the folks back home, who had probably received copies of our itinerary, might have concerns.

The wraith shook his head once then drifted through the closed door into the hall. Linus opened it, and we found Cletus posted outside our room in a forbidding black cloud of menace.

"Fine," I grumbled half-heartedly for show. "You can stay."

With a sigil to give Linus and me privacy, I could live with it. As long as Cletus stayed out here, I doubted Linus would mind either. He tended toward overprotectiveness, and we *were* hunting a violent spirit.

Cletus trailed his icy fingers across my cheek, and I leaned into his touch.

Down deep, he embodied what remained of Maud. I couldn't take offense at Cletus wanting to watch over me, over *us*, but no one wanted to bring their mom along on their honeymoon.

The romance of the moment had spluttered and died a sexually frustrating death, so I gave up on manhandling my new husband in favor of getting us unpacked. Just in case anyone slipped in, either to maul us or perform maid services, I wanted to get anything questionable locked behind wards.

Linus joined me after shutting out Cletus, and we finished the job together. All domestic-like.

"You brought your full kit," I commented on the contents at the bottom of his suitcase. Everything he might need for any number of supernatural emergencies was right there.

Trailing his fingers over the ratty backpack in mine, the seventh or eighth I'd purchased since accepting the title of Potentate of Savannah, he smiled. "You also brought yours."

"Yeah, well." I swatted away his hand. "The guy who trained me was a real stickler."

The truth was, I had fallen into the routine of protecting my city day in and day out, and I felt naked without the tools of my trade.

And the city? I missed her with a bone-deep ache. The bond between us stretched too taut to vibrate, and the stillness within left me twitchy. Empty in a way I hadn't been since bonding with her.

But this was my honeymoon, and even potentates deserved a week off now and again.

Not even a week. Barely a long weekend. And that included the travel here and back.

It was the longest either of us could afford to spend away from our respective duties.

Savannah would just have to understand. Too bad I couldn't bring her back a *My Potentate Honeymooned in a Haunted House and All I Got was This Lousy Shirt* tee to smooth things over, but the city was a bit large to tarp in cotton.

Making a production of dusting my hands, I surveyed the room. "Now what?"

A mischievous smile curved his lips as he palmed the rental car key fob. "You'll see."

THREE

The library closed at five according to the sun-bleached sign taped to the corrugated siding. *Library* was a noble title for the sagging heap before us. A singlewide trailer the size of a shipping container leaned away from crumbling red concrete stairs leading to a door that might have been the same color before water damage caused the paint to flake. The poor thing had been parked in a graveled lot overgrown with weeds and forgotten by the looks of it.

The only recent signs of life were across the street where a bright yellow backhoe huddled next to three blue dump trucks as if afraid of the dark. The parcel where they sat must have been a quarry, but the sign at the road was too faded to read the details. Only the gaping holes left in the earth behind them spoke to the nature of the business.

"I enjoy bedtime reading as much as the next girl, but what are we doing here?"

"We're going to check the archives." He walked up the steps without tottering, even when they rocked beneath him on the uneven ground. "The librarian was polite when I called, but Ms. Ayer blames the internet for the decline of the library system." He used a sigil to pop the lock with the ease of a seasoned breaker-and-enterer. "She refused to email me copies of the articles pertaining to Oliphant House."

"Ah."

Noticing my confusion, he explained, "The town paper shared a building with the library."

"Ah," I said again, meaning it this time. "That's where the archives come in. Gotcha."

After he switched on the light, I followed him into a cramped and musty space plastered in vintage book posters. Shelves lined all the walls, and they sagged beneath the weight of their burdens and a healthy coating of dust.

The lone computer hulked on a tattered desk at the rear of the building. The monitor was yellowed with age, and it would have taken both of us to lift it. The keyboard was clunky, the letters rubbed away, and the mouse anchored to a cord the width of a number two pencil.

Linus aimed straight for it, sat in the child-sized chair, and booted up the computer.

"You said *shared*. Past tense." I stood behind him. "What happened? Did the paper give the library the boot?"

"Arson." He leaned forward when the screen flickered with its first sign of life. "The building burned to the ground eighteen years ago." He began typing at the prompt. "What you see is all that remains of the library's original inventory plus donations and whatever else they were able to purchase with the remainder of the small grant they received to buy this trailer."

The floors squished underfoot when I shifted my weight. "They never rebuilt?"

"There was no money for it in the town budget."

"What happened to the newspaper?"

"The family took the insurance money and moved to Florida." He clicked around until he found what we came to retrieve. "All that remains of their one-hundred-and-thirty-eight-year run is on this computer."

That was roughly four or five anniversaries' worth of information. "How did those records survive?"

"The great-great-grandson of the paper's founder had begun a project to preserve the family's legacy two years prior to the fire. He transferred all the microfiche and surviving paper copies from the library to his basement, where he scanned them into a database. He donated a duplicate of that information to the library since they shared such a long history with the paper, but he kept the originals."

"Lucky."

"I'm sure Ms. Ayer would disagree."

"You know what I mean." I pushed his shoulder. "Smarty-pants."

Once upon a time, he would have flinched away from the gentle tease, but he had toughened up after enduring my twisted sense of humor for so long.

"Can you turn on the printer?" Linus sank back into his research. "I've located the files we need, but there's nowhere to insert the thumb drive I brought."

On a file cabinet behind the librarian's desk, I spotted a printer as wide as a pizza box.

"Copies are twenty-five cents per page. That's pretty steep." I flipped the switch, and it screeched with annoyance at having been woken in the middle of the night. "Can you afford it?"

"Do you accept credit or debit cards?"

"Nope." I rubbed my fingertips together. "This is a cash-only establishment."

"Then perhaps my wife will loan me the money."

"You're cute and all, but I can't afford to go around making loans willy-nilly." I gave him a stern look I ruined bending over to fish my emergency twenty from beneath the insole in my right sneaker. "You're going to have to work this off."

"I appreciate your generosity."

"I expect you to." I winked. "Later."

A flush spread across his cheeks, turning them red beneath his freckles, and I struggled against the desire to gather his face between my palms and kiss him until neither of us could breathe.

Someday it would get old. Maybe. Knowing I wasn't alone in the world anymore. But I hoped the day was long in coming when I no longer experienced that giddy thrill each time he slid on his glasses or smiled at me with his eyes over their rims.

I wanted us to stay this way forever, not long at all.

Linus straightened from his hunched position and studied the door. "Do you hear that?"

"Over this?" The printer at my hip rattled, thumped, and shook. "Nope."

As I dismissed it, the building swayed and then fell still. I checked to make sure I hadn't leaned against the counter, that the printer wasn't playing tricks on me, but I hadn't, and it wasn't.

Rising slowly, Linus crept to the door and gripped its dented knob.

He twisted it, threw his shoulder into it, then faced me with a line carved between his brows.

"That is not your happy face." I scooped up the warm pages as the printer wheezed into silence, an easy task since it was the perforated type you had to tear at the top and bottom to separate. "What's going on out there?"

"I'm not sure." He took a step back, and black swallowed his eyes from corner to corner. The room dimmed as my vision did the same. "The door is wedged shut."

Cletus lent us his vision as he materialized in the parking lot with an air of *I told you so.*

The yellow backhoe had been driven across the road, and its arm extended against the door. That's what pinned us in. The driver was dressed in black from head to toe and wore a mask that left only the slits of their eyes visible. The wannabe arsonist also held two Molotov cocktails primed and ready to go.

"What are you waiting for?" I gave Cletus a panicked jolt. "Take them down."

The wraith didn't give them time to work on their aim. He knocked the bottles from their hands with an effort of will, and the glass shattered on the gravel. Fire whooshed out, devoured the fuel, then spluttered and died.

Spinning a quick circle, the figure searched for their assailant. Almost falling when they spotted Cletus, they gasped a panicked noise then sprinted down the road to where they must have parked their getaway vehicle.

"That's one crisis averted." I sagged against Linus. "Now at least we won't be flambéed."

Cletus gave chase for about a mile before circling back, afraid to leave us unprotected.

"Too bad he can't drive." I pressed my ear against the wood. "The engine is still running."

Wraiths were like poltergeists in that they could manifest, but they didn't have much finesse. I had seen Cletus rip out a vampire's trachea with a vicious swipe of his claws but drop a crust of bread to feed Keet so many times he descended into frenzy and left crumbs behind. Which, to be honest, Keet didn't mind.

"We'll have to let ourselves out, I'm afraid." Linus cast his gaze around the room before settling on the door. "We need to hurry in case our arsonist friend keeps a change of pants in his trunk."

Cletus did tend to have that effect on people who could see him. I had almost peed my pants more than once after he startled me with a sudden appearance.

"What are you thinking?" No windows meant no glass to break, and there was only one door. Talk about your fire hazards. "We're pretty well stuck."

"Can you locate a sigil that might help?"

With the Marchand collection at my disposal, I didn't have to rely on genetic memory these days. I studied, practiced, and generally busted my butt to master my brand of magic. But there were still times, like this one, when I was forced to dig deeper than the written word to what lingered on the periphery of my thoughts.

Closing my eyes, I focused on the problem and waited until a sigil presented itself to me. I turned the design over in my head, examining it, but it was a new one on me. Certain I had committed it to memory, I opened my eyes.

"Here goes nothing." I pushed out a breath and sliced open my finger. I drew the sigil on the door then gave it a second. "Hmm." The design pulsed once then began to erase itself from the outside in. "That's...weird."

Linus bent his head to examine it, but his expression cleared before the design vanished altogether.

"*Oomph.*"

I hit the carpet with a dull thud, Linus on top of me, just as the sequence completed.

An explosion rocked the building, and smoke poured into the room until the air blackened.

"Well, that was unexpected." I coughed as he rolled off me. "What's the damage?"

Rising into a crouch, he squinted through the haze. "You blew a hole in the door."

"I'm guessing Ms. Ayer won't love me for that."

"Probably not."

Linus gave me a hand up, and we went to inspect the damage. The hole was large enough that either of us could have fit through it, but I made the executive decision that he could go because boobs.

Thanks to a steady diet of Vitamin L infused smoothies, and anything involving bacon, chocolate, or chocolate-covered bacon, I had a lusher figure these days. I finally had my curves back, but that meant ceding ground in covert operations to those who could fit through doggy-door-sized holes without sucking in their stomachs.

As much as the view tempted me, I didn't even pinch his butt on his way out.

Granted, I immediately regretted the decision once he stood on the other side.

A minute or two later, the building swayed again, and I tested the crumpled door.

As I stepped out, Linus climbed down from the backhoe with grease on his hands.

"Hot-wired." He removed a handkerchief from his pocket and wiped himself clean. "Not well either."

"It still got the job done." I called the cleaners on our way to the car with the address and made a mental note to donate funds anonymously to the struggling library. It was the least I could do for blowing it up a little. "Do you think they followed us from the inn?"

"It seems likely." He held the door for me then rounded the car and got in. "I don't have many business dealings this far north. I'm not aware of any enemies we, or the Society, have in the area."

"Whoever is responsible must have noticed us checking in and was also informed enough to guess why we paid the library a visit."

"That's a big leap."

"True." I wiggled my feet in the floorboard. "And yet, my legs aren't even tired."

Amusement kindled in his eyes as I settled in with the information that had almost cost us our lives.

Two pages in, I stumbled across the first red flag and checked it against other records in the stack.

"No strange deaths in or on the Oliphant property so far, but entire families go missing like clockwork in this town and the surrounding areas during the week of the cycle. There are several stories featuring the mysterious disappearances."

"Any commonalities?"

"Aside from the fact they were all tourists? None that I can see." I compared the lists. "Married couples and their kids, single mothers and their kids, widows and their kids…" I exhaled slowly. "Kids are definitely a theme, but the oldest accounts are framed as 'Mr. So and So, his wife, and their children' without much in the way of details. Without those, we can't draw any links between gender or age."

"We can't connect them to the inn, either." He flipped on the blinker, turning into the driveway leading us back to Oliphant House. "Guests who were attacked might have required medical intervention, but they checked out of the inn with a pulse."

"Hmm." I spared a glance through the windshield as the inn came into view but returned to my research with an inward grin at the monster Linus had created when he assigned me all that homework. "There's one mention of a death involving both a missing tourist and Oliphant House." I eyeballed the date with a frown. "Looks recent." I double-checked the information on my phone. "As in the last cycle recent."

"This person died on the property?" Concern pleated his brow. "Are you sure?"

"A husband and wife with a newborn son were abducted from their hotel room in town. The husband put up a good fight. There was blood spatter on the rug and bedspread." I switched back to my phone. "He was later found decapitated on the far edge of the Oliphant property." I wrinkled my nose. "When I say *he*, I mean *his head*. It was in a plastic grocery bag. The body was never located. Neither were his wife or their child."

"Perhaps we ought to walk the property." He drummed the wheel with his fingertips. "Get the lay of the land."

The car rocked when he came to a stop, and motion drew my eye to the cottage behind the inn. The Oliphants sat on their back porch, which faced us, with steaming mugs in their hands. We waved as we exited the vehicle, and they waved back. I worried they might have something on their minds, given they had waited up for us, but they appeared content to let us resume our honeymoon activities without interference.

"They keep late hours," I observed on our way in. "So much for taking a late-night stroll."

"They must have noticed us leaving." He led the way to the kitchen, familiar with my bedtime-snack routine. "There seems to be a lot of that going around."

The fact our hosts were wide awake nearing three in the morning spoke to either odd sleeping habits or curiosity. Neither would make our time here go smoothly if we got caught sticking our noses where they didn't belong.

"I'm tired, so I'm going to pretend—just for tonight—that they were waiting up for us out of a sense of obligation and not for sinister reasons."

As owners of a haunted house, little old lady and gent or not, the sinister vibe was unavoidable.

With that happy thought circling my brain, I doubled back and peeked out the window to find the Oliphants standing shoulder to shoulder, gazing out into the night toward the inn.

Not creepy at all.

No siree.

Trailing after Linus, I explored the kitchen. It was nothing fancy or industrial. The two bulky stainless fridges were its only obvious concession to the B&B lifestyle. I crossed to one then snooped to my heart's content. I located a carton of bright-red strawberries ripe to bursting, stole the whole thing, and bit into the topmost one with a happy groan.

Amusement twitching in his cheeks, Linus wiped the juice from my chin. "I don't smell anything offensive, do you?"

"No." I tossed the leafy bit in the trash. "Bread and onions, definitely. Maybe hamburgers. Collards. Oh! I bet it was cornbread and meatloaf with greens on the side."

"You spend far too much time with Lethe if you can divine their menu from a sniff."

Seeds and all, I flashed him my teeth in a gwyllgi-worthy smile.

"The basement entrance is located in the pantry, according to the blueprints I found online." He checked the knob and found it locked. "Do you want to explore it tonight or save it for tomorrow?"

"I don't want to use up my quotient for fun on the first night." I rubbed my shoulder where it throbbed from where Linus pushed me to the floor in the library. "We'll pick the lock after breakfast like civilized people."

Curious if any missing persons had been reported in the area, Linus put in a call to the team at the Office of the Potentate of Atlanta. With that done, we burned up the predawn hours exploring the inn.

The magic in the air came and went, no stronger in any one part of the house than another. It permeated the walls, the floors, the ceilings. Everything. I tried and failed to track it a few times, but it vanished before I traced it to its source.

Snacking as I went, I hesitated on the threshold to the study. "How long did you say we have before the murderversary?"

"Wouldn't our earlier findings make it a maulaversary? Or perhaps a demonversary?"

"Nah." I reached into the carton but came up empty. "Murderversary is catchier, plus the severed head totally qualifies it."

"Two days left." He entered the room behind me. "I thought you would appreciate the ticking-clock aspect."

"You're really getting into this." I tossed the empty carton into the trash. "I had no idea you enjoyed playing Sherlock Holmes so much."

"And I had no idea you could devour an entire carton of strawberries without a chocolate chaser." He pressed his lips to the top of my head. "We're still learning all sorts of interesting things about one another." His kisses drifted lower, turned slower. "So far, we've checked into our suite, almost gotten checked out at the library, and depleted the fresh fruit stores. What's next?"

"I left the rest of my ideas up in our room. Specifically, on the bed. Come with me, and I'll show them to you."

The pinkening skin beneath his freckles made me want to taste them, but there was no rush. For once, it was just the two of us—plus Cletus—and we had nowhere to be and nothing to do but love one another.

And, you know, hope we didn't get maimed or murdered in our sleep.

FOUR

The creak and groan of old wood broke Linus's concentration. He glanced up from his book to check and see if Grier had heard what sounded like footsteps on the stairs, but her eyes were shut, her lips slightly parted. The clock on the nightstand flashed the time in red numbers. Just after dusk. Most necromancers would still be sleeping at this hour. Most, but not all. Not him.

Setting his e-reader aside, he slid out of bed and padded across the room. Careful not to wake her, he exited into the hall and shut the door behind him. He drew a protective sigil on the frame with his modified pen before going to investigate.

This particular phenomenon was a well-documented one, but he had never experienced it for himself. Intrigued, he walked the length of the hall to the stairs and waited with his ears primed for the slightest noise. He could see ghosts, but not all ghosts could be seen. Residuals weren't powerful enough. They were mere echoes of past events, usually traumas, doomed to repeat forever as flashes, scents, or noises.

Positioned as he was, he kept an eye on the door leading to their room as well as on the stairs. It was his attention on the bedroom that earned him his first glimpse of the otherworldly since their arrival.

A long shadow broke from the darkness clinging to the corners and took a step toward the door. The instant it made contact with the sigil, it shrieked in a high-pitched yowl that raised the hairs down his nape. Whirling on him, the thing identified the true danger and hissed, baring tiny fangs.

Hands in his pockets, calm mask in place, Linus strolled toward it. "Who are you?"

The creature snarled and spat but made no intelligible sounds.

Having performed an exorcism or two in his day, he moved down the list. "Why are you here?"

Curling in on itself, it dug into the pockets of darkness around it as if searching for the hole it came through.

Close enough to catch a whiff of brimstone, the rotten-egg scent Kylie had complained about, Linus wished for his phone and its flashlight. "What do you want?"

A keening noise rose from the creature, who hunched as small as it could get.

Peculiar behavior for a ghost and far too skittish to be a poltergeist. "Are you...afraid?"

The thing blinked at him then, its eyes yellow and its pupils elongated, as if it understood him.

A sharp slice of pain swiped him from shoulder to hip, and Linus spun to find another creature in retreat. Reaching behind him, he touched his back, and his fingers came away bloody. When he turned to check on the original creature, it was gone.

"Interesting." Giving the hall one last glance, he murmured, "Very interesting."

Grier woke as the door to their suite shut behind him, and she snuggled deeper under the covers. "Hi."

"Hello." He approached the bed. "Did you sleep well?"

"I was out like a light." She twisted onto her side toward him. "Did I miss anything?"

"Footsteps on the stairs and this." He untucked his shirt, exposing his back. "What do you make of it?"

The yawn stretching her mouth transformed into a gasp. "What happened?"

Grier shoved the quilts aside and rose onto her knees, hauling him close to examine the wounds.

"I met one of our resident spooks." He probed the edges with his fingers. "How does it look?"

"Honestly? Like a cat scratched you." She popped his hand to get him out of her way. "There are five rows." She traced the curve of muscle beneath them. "The centermost ones are deepest." She mapped the length of them with her fingertips. "The reach is impressive. No house cat could have done this."

"It hissed and spat at me." He let her guide him onto the bed on his stomach. "Its eyes were feline as well." Her warm fingers traveled over him, and his gut tightened beneath her touch. "The one I saw, anyway."

Her exploration paused. "There's more than one?"

"Apparently so."

"That wasn't in the brochure," she murmured. "I'm taking a reference photo, and then I'm healing this."

"It doesn't hurt."

"You could be missing your spine, and you'd still claim it didn't hurt." She slapped him on the butt, and he didn't mind the sting. "You have to take better care of yourself."

Several clicks later, she had their evidence recorded on her phone.

"Hold still." She straddled his hips and yanked the cap off her modified pen. "This won't take but a second."

The tickle of the pen nib sent skitters racing over his skin, but there was no familiar tingle from her magic.

"Um." She traced the bottommost scratch with her finger. "This isn't healing."

Cranking his head toward her, he soaked up her adorable bafflement. "There must be a toxin."

The analgesic qualities of some venoms might explain why it didn't hurt as much as it perhaps should.

"Of course, there is." She blasted out a sigh. "You get in the worst trouble when left unsupervised."

The same was true of her, but even a new husband knew when to keep his mouth shut.

"I'll have to break out the big guns." She sat back, and her weight shifted. "Hold very, very still."

Linus shut his eyes and rested his chin on top of his hands where they were folded in front of him.

"Ready?"

"Yes."

The blade of his old pocketknife *snicked* free of its handle, and Linus caught the faintest whiff of copper.

Murmuring softly, she painted his back with the warmth of her blood. The gentle caresses told him she was outlining each scratch to ensure maximum coverage. With that done, she pressed her palms flat against his shoulder blades and pushed magic into him with effort that left her trembling.

Pins and needles stabbed him, and a bubbly sensation filled his stomach. His skin took on a luminescent quality, and he turned his hand this way and that. He never grew tired of watching Grier work her brand of magic. It amazed him, even now, what miracles she could perform.

"Ha." She bent down and kissed his spine. "All better."

"Thank you."

"Well?" She leaned forward to check in. "How does it feel?"

"The pain is gone." He twisted around to face her. "Do you think it will scar?"

A reminder of the incident didn't bother him, but it was a gauge to hold up against how powerful the toxin must have been.

"Normally? Yeah." She ducked to kiss his cheek. "But you won't."

Warmth that had nothing to do with her magic spread through his chest until it hurt to breathe. "I love you."

"Hmm." She pretended to consider him. "I suspected as much."

Happy to play along, he asked, "How could you tell?"

"Oh, you know. Feeding me, saving my life, feeding me, seducing me with your freckles, feeding me. Then there was the whole agreeing-to-marry-me thing."

"How did I seduce you with my freckles?"

"They're just there." She pointed a damning finger at his nose. "All adorable and kissable."

A frown pinched his forehead. "That counts as seduction?"

"I have trouble keeping my hands to myself around you." She folded her arms over her chest. "Whose fault do you think that is, *Mr. Woolworth*?"

With a calculated twist of his hips, Linus flipped Grier onto her side then her back and climbed over her. "Not mine."

"Are you implying it's *my* fault that *you* are so gorgeous I can't stop touching you?" She widened her eyes. "How rude."

"No one else thinks I'm gorgeous." He smiled down at her. "Perhaps you should borrow my glasses."

"Pfft." She jabbed him in the ribs with her thumbs until he laughed. "You're not that blind."

"No one saw me until you." He slid the length of her dark hair through his fingers. "Others wanted my title, my fortune, or my influence. No one wanted me." He closed his fist around the silky strands. "No one but you."

"People are dumb." She cradled his face in her palm. "Trust me, I was dumb for a long time too."

The reminder her heart had once belonged wholly to Boaz Pritchard throbbed like a sore tooth at the oddest times, but it had grown fainter over the years. The ring on Linus's finger had helped more than the passage of time. His wedding band was a tangible reminder that Grier had made her choice for all to see.

A loud crash followed by a dull thump brought her jerking

upright, almost unseating him, and an eager glint kindled in her eyes. "Let's go see what we see."

Linus rolled aside and pulled on dress shoes while she wriggled into holey jeans, a faded tee, and broken-in sneakers.

Out in the hall, he gave the corner where the creature had cowered a long look, but there was no hint of it now. The stairs, which had failed to produce anything of consequence earlier, provided them with an answer for the ruckus.

In a tumble of limbs at the bottom sat Kylie. Dressed all in shades of blue, she had layered her clothes for an ombré effect similar to yesterday's ensemble. Her hoodie concealed her face, and she brandished her flashlight like a weapon until she could shove back the fabric and gain her bearings.

"Goddess," Grier breathed. "Are you all right?"

"Yeah." Kylie jerked at the sound of Grier's voice, startled. "I'm good."

Grier hit the stairs at a clip, and Linus followed close in case whatever shoved Kylie tried again with Grier.

"Don't move." Linus knelt beside the teen. "Let me check to see if anything is broken."

The tension in her body shouted a warning she didn't handle touch well. "Are you really a doctor?"

His medical training was more than sufficient to care for a human. "Yes."

With as little contact as possible, he coached her through a few movements to determine whether she had broken or sprained anything during her fall. From what he could tell without closer examination, she was lucky to have escaped with a bump where her forehead hit the railing.

Grier, who hovered behind him, rested her hands on his shoulders. "What are you doing here?"

"I..." Kylie worried the piercing in her lip but must have remembered what Grier told her about Linus being more willing to pay for honesty. "Things aren't great at home. Mom has her panties in a wad about her boyfriend running off with her best friend, who she stole him from in the first place. Grams and Gramps are cool, but I hate putting them in the middle." She sighed. "I come here to hang out when there are no guests. There were only two of you, so I figured I could stay out of your way. I didn't mean for you to know I was here."

At check-in, Kylie had implied she lived in the cottage behind the inn with her grandparents. Her mother wasn't mentioned. Granted, she could have moved home, or perhaps she never left, but Kylie's fidgeting made him wonder if she wasn't editing her story to fit her audience.

Grier, who tightened her grip on him, put the most pressing question to Kylie gently. "How did you fall?"

"The ghost shoved me." She glared at the staircase. "Again."

"Can you remember if anything about this time was different from the last?"

"Yeah." Her Adam's apple bobbed. "A voice whispered in my ear."

We waited for her to elaborate, but she burst into wild laughter.

"You should see your faces." She cackled. "You totally believe this stuff is real."

The stuff totally was real, but Linus had no intention of sparking that debate.

"I tripped over my shoelaces." She tucked her legs under her. "One must have come untied."

This incident discredited her earlier confessions, and she must have worried we would ask for a refund.

"The other stuff was true, though." She pushed to her feet, expression earnest. "Promise."

"Mm-hmm." Grier shook her head. "You can stay here tonight, but you need to be gone in the morning."

"You must know the lore," Linus said, rising. "I doubt we're the first to mention it."

"We get morbids in here all the time. Folks pay extra for the rooms with the most activity."

That might explain the markup on their room, given its proximity to the stairs. Though Mr. Oliphant had given him a discounted rate after he made it clear he wanted the entire inn at their disposal.

Linus raised his eyebrows. "Morbids?"

"Folks who get off on death, the occult, whatever." She eyed him up and down. "I pegged you for one the second you got out of your fancy rental." She flicked a glance at Grier, who was arguably the most powerful necromancer of their time. "You seem nice. What are you doing with this guy?"

The expression Grier wore got stuck between amusement and insult and stayed there.

"Are you even married?" Kylie narrowed her eyes on Linus. "Is this really your honeymoon?"

"Yes and yes," Grier answered for him. "And if you ever want to see another dollar from us, you'll watch your mouth when you talk to or about my husband." Grier's eyes brightened on the word, and her joy was contagious. "Now shoo. Back to your room."

"Fine."

Kylie tromped upstairs without another misstep, and they watched her go, just in case.

"We've got time before the big day." Grier stared in the direction the girl had gone. "She ought to be safe here for one night." She shook her head. "Something tells me that teen is going to be trouble."

Linking their fingers, they walked into the kitchen together. "Something tells me you're right."

FIVE

As I was wont to do, I snooped more while Linus puttered around in the kitchen. After our run-in with Kylie, he had added a sigil to the door of the second refrigerator to keep any unsuspecting humans out of our groceries. There was blood in there, his, and it would be a teensy bit hard to explain if Kylie got the munchies and rooted through our supplies accidentally on purpose.

Then again, she already thought we were morbids, a term I hadn't heard in ages, so she might expect us to travel with chicken blood for satanic rituals.

Kids these days.

They had no proper occult education.

The pantry drew my attention time and again until I couldn't resist the urge to tinker. "Do you mind if I get cracking on this lock?"

"Not at all." He mashed a button on the blender, adding strawberries from a second carton into my nightly Vitamin L smoothie.

Pen in hand, I skimmed my memory then drew on a complex sigil that would work best. I pushed magic into the design, and it popped the lock with a satisfying *snick*. Eager as I was to get going, I left it intact until Linus could join me.

"Ready when you are," I called, wiping off the sigil with a damp cloth in case we had more unexpected visitors. Say, apologetic grandparents or a harried mother searching for our stowaway.

Linus appeared at my shoulder, smoothie in hand, and watched me drink the first course of my breakfast like a good little half-vampire. And no, the need for blood and the truth of my parentage never got any less weird. Neither did the infrequent urge to drink straight from the tap.

Nutella-filled crepes topped with whipped cream and chopped hazelnuts came next, along with a side order of bacon. The dish was one of my favorite indulgences, and he was spoiling me rotten. As usual.

We cleaned up after ourselves and got ready to begin our adventure.

"Hellmouth, here we come." I rubbed my hands together and drew open the pantry door. "Oh. Hrm."

The pantry was a perfect cube of floor-to-ceiling shelves with an open door opposite the entrance.

The faintest whiff of sulfur tickled my nose from the yawning dark, and I almost sneezed twice.

"Why lock the pantry but not the basement?" I entered the small room. "Why leave this ajar?"

"Doors that open and shut on their own are a prerequisite for a haunted house," he murmured, leaning around me for a clearer view. "You're not getting spooked, are you?"

"Are you serious?" Grinning, I held up my arm to show off my goose bumps. "This is freaky as heck."

Demons, the type from Christian hell, didn't exist as far as I knew. That didn't mean the lore didn't come from somewhere. There were creatures aplenty in the world we shared with humans, and that didn't take fae into consideration. They came in as many and as varied forms as anything born of Earth.

The possibilities were literally endless.

"As long as you're enjoying yourself," he said, planting a kiss on my temple.

"This is going to be epic." I took out my phone and flicked on the flashlight. "It's also going to be dark." I shined the beam across the walls to either side of the rickety stairs. "I don't see a light switch, do you?"

"Look up."

"Well shoot."

A single bulb had once hung above the top step, the simple kind of light you clicked on and off with a tug on a beaded chain. All that remained was a handful of wires where someone had yanked it out of the ceiling.

"Good thing we've got the advantage." I tested the top step. "We should be okay."

Necromancers came standard with excellent night vision. The light from our phones would be plenty to allow our eyes to adjust to the gloom once we got down there. And if we needed more, that could be arranged too.

"The blueprints indicate the basement itself is average." Linus slid past me, slick as spit, then reached back for my hand. "Things don't get peculiar until you reach the first subbasement."

After he switched his phone's flashlight on, he led us down. The space looked about how you might expect, except for its old wooden floors. I had never seen those in a basement. Only dirt or concrete. Then again, I had never been in a house built on top of a maze leading to the theoretical underworld.

"Do you smell that?" I wrinkled my nose but kept following the scent. "It's coming from over here."

The exterior walls were made from old brick, but the straight lines were broken in one corner where the neat rows deviated into an arch. A door appeared to be half buried, stuck between floors. No hardware was visible, and I wondered if it opened. There was only one way to find out.

"Do you see those marks?" Linus indicated rows of deep scratches across the planks nearest the door.

"They resemble the ones on your back." I took a quick picture to add to our file. "Hard to tell if they were made by multiple creatures or the same one making repeated trips."

"There are at least two," Linus reminded me. "There could be more."

Bending over, I pressed two fingers against the door, and it swung wide. "Well, hello."

"There's enough room for an adult to squeeze through, but bare-ly." Linus eyed the resulting hole with distrust. "Are you sure you want to go down?"

"Are you serious?" I snort-laughed. "I'll flip a coin to see who goes first."

"Cletus." He waited for the wraith to manifest. "Search the area beyond the door. Make sure it's safe."

If you asked me, Cletus was throwing off smug vibes. The kind that said *I knew you would be lost without me.* That sense of self was unheard of in a wraith, but I wasn't complaining. Maud had been an opinionated woman. He was continuing the family tradition.

The wraith returned minutes later and gestured toward the opening with a long limb.

"Go on." Linus angled his light for me. "Just be careful. Please."

I planted a quick smooch on him then lowered onto my stomach and shimmied backward into the hole. Not gonna lie. I never would have done it without Cletus watching my back. Awkward as it might be honeymooning with three, it had its benefits too.

Once my feet hit another wooden floor, I stood back to give Linus room to join me.

The walls were coated in splotchy plaster that had crumbled onto the floors, leaving behind a chalky residue pocked with foot—and paw—prints. Linus read the spirits as feline, and he was seldom wrong. That meant we were dealing with catlike beasts who weren't afraid of humans, or else they wouldn't have ventured upstairs. And someone or something else. The fabled demon? Or perhaps the Oliphants?

Linus's feet hit the planks beside me, and he dusted off his tailored shirt with a frown for its stains. Or the stink. It was hard to tell. They were both equally offensive.

"Your friends have been through here." I flashed my light across the marks. "This place reeks, but it's not the rotten-egg smell from the pantry."

Ghosts didn't poop, though poltergeists had been known to fling it, so our suspect pool was growing shallower.

"Whatever they are, they've been denning down here for a long time." He pointed out piles of shredded fabric, what might be old nests made out of curtains or sheets from fifty or sixty years ago based on the design and the state of decay. "How are they accessing the inn?"

Using my modified pen, I drew a sigil for light on my palm and gave my phone a rest. I didn't need a new light source so much as I worried about the battery. If we got stuck down here, in this rickety wooden construct, I wanted every ounce of juice I could squeeze out of it to dial 911.

"The basement door was open," I reminded him. "Either they can go incorporeal, or someone is letting them in and out."

The figure in the library parking lot came to mind. That person had been able to perceive Cletus, so the shadow cats ought to be visible to them too. But we hadn't stumbled across anyone but Kylie in the inn. As much as she enjoyed mocking visiting ghost hunters, she struck me as a devout nonbeliever.

"The latter would mean we're dealing with two distinct creatures."

"Maybe the Oliphants are involved." It was worth throwing out there. "That would give us a classic creature/human combo."

"There are traces of magic," Linus said, dusting off his hands, "but the Oliphants are human."

"How sure are we?" I had been too busy wrapping my head

around our plot-twist honeymoon to pay much attention to our hosts. "There are charms and spells that can alter a person, or creature, enough to pass for someone or something else."

Thanks to my former best friend, Amelie, I knew that for a certainty. So did Linus, who had aided in her transformation.

"We can perform a simple test if we find them in the house."

"Works for me." I ventured deeper into the hallway. "We should add Kylie to that list while we're at it."

"I agree." He pocketed his phone and held out his palm. "Would you mind?"

Linus was more than capable of activating a simple light sigil, but it warmed me from tip to toe that he preferred I do the honors.

"You're getting spoiled." I clucked my tongue. "There was a time when you worried a light sigil from me would set you on fire."

"There was a time when I thought sweater vests were the height of fashion."

Smothering a snort of laughter, I drew the design, and illumination burst from his palm. "There you go."

The sigils provided more than enough light for our vision to adjust, but the deeper we traveled, the more peculiar and precarious the landscape grew. The wood was in decent shape despite its age, but the floors were buckled, and the brittle planks groaned to accept an ounce more weight.

How did the Oliphants sleep at night knowing their guests perched on the edge of this yawning abyss?

Lost in contemplation about the potential for lawsuits, I tripped and almost face-planted into a wall.

"You've got to be kidding me." I kicked a pile of extension cords snaking in every direction. "What are these doing down here?"

"Let's find out, shall we?" Linus lifted one of the orange strands and followed it to where it plugged into a cracked outlet protruding from the wall. "I didn't expect that."

"Who puts an outlet in a maze?" I crouched to examine it. "See this?" I pointed out the dueling cartoon monsters plated in heavy battle armor on the outlet cover. "I remember when this cartoon released. It was a favorite of mine when I was a kid. That means this cover was added in the last fifteen years or so."

"The wiring could be older." Linus pulled a multipurpose tool from his pocket, which had replaced the knife I had stolen, and used its screwdriver attachment to remove the plate and get a peek at its guts. "Aluminum wiring. That dates it from the sixties to the seventies."

"Aluminum wiring is bad, right?"

"Yes." He replaced the cover. "Whoever has been using this outlet recently has been overloading it." He pointed out scorch marks on the wall. "It's a miracle they haven't burned the house down around them."

"It's a pile of kindling," I agreed. "I'm amazed there's no water damage."

Basements were notorious for flooding and moisture problems in our neck of the woods. Maybe this far north it wasn't as big of an issue. Even with the brick perimeter shoring up the house's foundation, I figured there would be more rot or mold, but this level was in decent condition. The next...who knew?

"The lower levels will tell." He mirrored my thoughts. "Do you want to go deeper?"

"Do you think it's safe?" The wiring worried me more than the creatures. "How accurate are the blueprints you found?"

"I believe we'll be safe to go down another floor, maybe two. Beyond that, we'll have to ask Cletus to scout for us." He patted the pocket over his phone. "We can't trust the blueprints beyond that point. They've been online for too long. Anyone could have seeded fakes. The first three levels down are the only ones that match up across all the records I dug up on the house."

"Let's go then." I wished, just for a second, that Lethe were here. Her nose would have come in handy. So would her prey drive if these shadow cats proved to be tangible creatures rather than noncorporeal ones. "Lead the way."

We walked another fifteen minutes before Linus indicated a warped hatch in the floor with a frown.

"There are more cords here." He lifted the square of wood covered in nicks and shone his light down into the opening. "There's a ladder." He glanced up as the wraith appeared, no doubt summoned by his thoughts. "Well?"

Cletus drifted into the opening and performed his recon while Linus and I wondered at the modern touches to what he had been led to believe was a sealed relic from the inn's past.

A low moan drifted from the darkness, and Linus beat me to the ladder. I'm sure he would say he went first because he stood closer, but I saw the bounce in his steps as he tested each rung along the way. He could be so adorable at times.

"You're not going to believe this," he called up to me. "Someone has been living down here."

"You're right." I got down to his level. "I don't believe it."

Yet the evidence was scattered all around us. An inflatable mattress covered with rumpled modern sheets. A small flat screen TV fed into what appeared to be a Wi-Fi hub. A mini fridge stuffed with snacks and energy drinks. Clothes mounded in the corner, a rainbow of tees, jeans, hoodies, and sneakers in coordinating colors.

"This explains the open pantry door." I rubbed my forehead. "Kylie didn't say she stayed in a room at the inn. We made the assumption." Aided by her fall down the stairs. "She said she comes here to hang out when there are no guests, but she never told us where."

"Technically, she didn't lie." He picked up the drift of my thoughts. "She just didn't tell us the truth."

"She had to come up the stairs to fall down them," I pointed out. "If she wasn't staying in a room, she might have been spying on us."

Nodding, he thinned his lips. "She might be working with our arsonist friend."

"Heck." The cat burglar getup meant we hadn't seen their face. "She might *be* our arsonist friend."

A weighty sigh moved through his chest. "What must her home life be like if she finds this preferable?"

Kylie and her grandfather had appeared to be on good terms at check-in, but appearances could be deceiving. Sure, he slipped up on the pronoun, but he was quick to apologize, and Kylie had laughed it off. Still, there might be tension we didn't pick up on given the briefness of our interaction with them.

"A better question is how did these shadow cats get past her without her noticing?"

They would have made noise scrabbling through that door, the fact they roused Linus was proof of that. With the opening yards from her pillow, I couldn't see her sleeping through the racket. Each time she touched the trapdoor to open it, her fingers would have found the grooves left from their claws too.

"The family has never gone on record as being harmed." Linus didn't touch Kylie's things, but he examined them closely. "Perhaps the creatures are bound not to hurt her." He glanced back at me. "Human perception of the paranormal is thin. She might not be able to see the shadow cats. It would make sense if she blamed any noises on mice."

"It would clear her name as the arsonist too." I rubbed my arms. "If she can't see the cats, then she can't have seen Cletus."

"It appears as though you have chosen our method of testing the Oliphants."

Assuming they were human, they wouldn't be scarred for life by a visit from Cletus since he could drift right up to them and plant a kiss on their cheek without them noticing. Magic in the blood was required for that. However thin, however distant, it had to be there.

A distant thumping pounded out above us. "Do you hear that?"

"Too heavy to be footsteps." He straightened. "We should go." He took one final glance around the cluttered space. "The Oliphants might have returned to check on us, or to search for Kylie."

After last night, I got the feeling they kept a close eye on the inn during the anniversary week. It begged the question of why, if they were concerned for our safety, they kept it open. They must be confident of their debunking skills if more incidents came to light on their watch.

"Good call." I snapped a few shots, continuing our documentation of the phenomenon. "I get the impression they wouldn't be thrilled with us for breaking into their basement, let alone if they realized why we're really here."

There was also the risk they would find the basement door open and lock us in, but unless they had magic on their side, I wasn't too worried about them trapping us.

"The family has no official stance on the haunting or the attacks on guests." Linus gripped my hips and lifted me with preternatural strength, allowing me to haul myself one level higher with ease. "I doubt they would appreciate us poking into their family history."

Though he didn't need it, I still reached down for him. He clasped forearms with me and leapt, grasping the wood under my knees with his free hand. There was a time when he would have held his weight back from me and done it all himself, but I was slowly breaking him of his old habits.

Never again would he face an obstacle alone. That's what marriage meant to me, a partnership where burdens were distributed equally.

"They don't know what they're missing." I grunted when I helped tug him beside me. "The right promo can do a world of good for your business. To borrow from Kylie, morbids love this kind of stuff. There are plenty of folks who don't go for the hardcore hauntings but love to stay in a place where there's documented activity."

The documents, being witnessed by humans, were totally unreliable, but still. More bang for your advertising buck.

"Unless the family is involved." He stood and offered me his hand, pulling me to my feet. "Or was involved, originally. They might wish the inn's notoriety would fade."

"Nah." I shrugged when he glanced back at me. "At the very least, they're not discouraging the rumors. The family could have closed up shop this week, but they chose not to turn us away. We're talking generations who haven't had a moral problem with booking potential victims. They're cashing in whether they want to acknowledge it or not."

"I hadn't considered it in that light," he allowed. "I assumed they preferred to ignore the otherworldly aspect, as humans often do."

"Ignore it and maybe it will go away?"

"Precisely."

"There's the financial aspect too." I tended to remember that better than him. "It must cost a small fortune to keep a place this size running. Without capitalizing on its infamy, it might be hard keeping it booked in such a remote location."

The family, however unwitting they might be, were enabling the cycle just by keeping their doors open. One week every thirty years was hardly a crippling blow...unless you were already in financial straits. That might explain how they agreed to take Linus's money without losing sleep over possibly condemning guests to a mauling.

The noise amplified as we climbed higher, but it took me a second to grasp I wasn't hearing it through the walls. Cletus had gone to inspect on his own and was broadcasting the sound to Linus and me.

Whoever had come calling for us—I was still betting on a search party for Kylie—gave up halfway into our return trip to the surface. That suited me fine. I preferred a hot shower to entertaining hysterical relatives. But as I was imagining what Linus and I could get up to during said shower, we exited the subbasement into the basement, and the knocking resumed.

The *ignore it and maybe it will go away* school of thought definitely did not work for me.

We exited the pantry and shut it behind us, careful not to leave behind grimy handprints. There was no time to wash up first, so whoever out there was refusing to take the hint no one was home would have to suck it up and deal with the smell and the stains on us.

Linus beat me to the front door and opened it on a middle-aged couple dressed for square dancing. That was alarming enough, arriving in costume in the middle of the night, but their presence shot familiar tingles up my spine. The recognition was mutual, and their bright eyes goggled.

Vampires.

"You're L-L-Linus Lawson," the male stammered. "The Grande Dame's son."

"Actually," I chimed in, peeking over Linus's shoulder. "It's Linus Woolworth now."

"Grier Woolworth." The female dropped her jaw then elbowed her...mate? "That's Grier Woolworth." She dug in the purse hung on the crook of her arm. "Can we take a photo with you? Both of you?" She beamed up at us. "No one back home will ever believe us otherwise. What are you doing way out here?"

"We're on our honeymoon," Linus said smoothly, turning his head to kiss my cheek.

The vampires laughed and whooped at the joke, until they realized it wasn't one.

"Really?" The female deflated. "You could have gone anywhere in the world, and you ended up here?"

Before she injured Linus's feelings, I wedged myself in front of him. "Why don't you tell us more about why you're here?"

"Oh. Shoot." She clutched her phone to her chest. "I must have left my manners on the dance floor." She stuck out her hand. "I'm Barbara Rogoff, and this is my husband, Benny." She beamed as we shook. "Benny and Barb. That's what everyone calls us. You can too."

"Thanks." I retrieved my hand before she stuck it in her purse as a souvenir. "What did you say you're doing here?"

"We drop in every thirty years. The haunting, you know. That's why you're here, right? It must be." The glitter-flecked tassels on her skirt quivered with excitement. "I can't believe you're joining us."

Return trips to family-owned properties spaced thirty years apart were risky ventures. Humans aged plenty in that time. Vampires...not so much. Maybe that explained the wild getup. They must adopt a different persona each time and use a touch of vampire glamour to sell the fake identities.

"Barb." Benny placed a hand on her arm, cleared his throat, then addressed me. "We called to reserve a room and were told the inn was booked. We had a competition near here, so we figured it wouldn't hurt to drop by before we left the area."

Unless they were kicking up their heels in the local Food Saver parking lot, I had trouble believing that.

"Yours is the only car in the lot," she added, "so we thought we would knock and see if anything had changed."

"You're really here on your honeymoon?" He chuckled manfully. "She let you get away with that?"

"Benny." Barb paled, a neat trick for a vampire. "Don't forget who you're talking to, hon."

"Apologies," he said quickly. "We can wait for the next cycle." He shrugged. "We've got the time."

Square dancing vampire ghost hunters.

Now I had seen it all.

"Give us a minute." I shut the door and drew a privacy sigil on the frame with my pen. "What do you think?"

Linus furrowed his brow. "You're actually considering this?"

"Two potential suspects for our arsonist just fell into our lap, so yes."

"Bold move," he murmured, eyeing the door like he wanted to nail it shut.

"Desperate move," I countered. "Especially if they're worried that we'll solve the mystery and break the cycle."

Amusement looked good on him. "You think so?"

"I know so." I slid my hands around his hips and squeezed his butt because it was there, and it was mine, and why not? "Just think of the parades the locals will throw in our honor for ending the reign of terror."

"I would settle for sparing more human lives." His lips twitched. "Though a parade would be nice."

One of the things I loved most about Linus was the fact he was willing to play with me. He was rusty at first, and I stumped him on the regular even after years together, but he was getting better. More importantly, he was having fun too. I don't think he'd had nearly enough of that in his life until now.

"Remember you said that." I gave his buns a farewell pat. "I'll eat your half of the candy when they invite us to ride on the Local Saviors float."

"You're sure you want to do this?" He searched my face. "Can I be honest?"

Flattening my palm over his heart, I waited. "I prefer that, yes."

"I don't want to share you." He braced his forehead against mine. "This is one time I would rather look the other way."

"But you won't." His core of integrity was one of the things I admired about him. "Even if I offered you a free pass, you would still pursue this. It's who you are—who *we* are."

"You're right." A smile twitched at the corner of his mouth. "Let me pretend to be selfish a moment longer?"

"Take all the time you need." I tilted up my chin and kissed him. "The vampires have a history with the house. We can mine them for factual knowledge on the haunting." Excitement tingled in my fingertips. "Even if they're not our firebug, we've got a real shot at cracking this with their help."

"They are harder to kill than humans." He tugged a cobweb from my hair. "All right. Invite them in."

"For the record, we've done extensive testing on the privacy sigil. We're safe to have wild monkey sex in our room or any other room without vampire hearing picking up the details."

A flush turned his cheeks rosy. "Goddess, Grier."

"What?" I rubbed the sigil off the door. "You were thinking it too."

"I..." He cleared his throat. "Well, yes."

"You are the best thing that's ever happened to me." I kissed him long and soft. "I mean that."

A hitch in his voice betrayed him before he got out the words. "I know you do."

"They're so cute," Barb whisper-screamed to her husband as I opened the door. *"Adorable."*

Linus didn't squirm, but a lesser man might have in his shoes. Personally, I feared for his cheeks. Barb looked like a pincher.

Taking his hand, I gave it a squeeze. "You're welcome to stay with us."

"On the condition the Oliphants approve," he added. "This isn't our home to allow guests."

"I'll dial Mr. Oliphant up now." Benny performed a quick shuffle step. "This is fantastic."

"He's a new man once he straps on his dancing shoes." Barb shot me a wink. "He has moves."

Most vampires had better than human coordination and reflexes. Based on the sample, I wasn't sure if Benny got shorted or if he was that used to playing human when he got his boogie on.

Cletus appeared at my shoulder and set his hand there in a protective gesture.

"This is our wraith, Cletus." I patted his bony fingers. "He won't hurt you."

The widening of their eyes told me they for sure saw him, but that was to be expected with vampires.

"Best vacation ever," Barb squealed, spinning in a circle. "I can't believe our luck."

Asking a vampire their age was the height of rudeness, but I couldn't get a bead on these two. Their choice of extracurricular activities, plus their manners and excitability level slanted them toward the younger end of the spectrum, in vampire years. But there was a near tangible weight to their presence on my senses. Because there were two? Or because they were old? Hard to tell.

"Mr. Oliphant would like a word with you." Benny passed over the phone. "If you don't mind."

"Of course." Linus accepted the cell and conducted a low conversation with the innkeeper.

"He's so elegant." Barb sighed after Linus turned his back. "I've seen pictures, but wow. He reminds me of the porcelain dolls my grandmother used to keep seated at her formal dining room table. Perfect hair, perfect clothes." She touched the golden cowboy boot charm on her necklace. "We weren't allowed to play with them." Her mouth thinned. "There was always something so sad about that."

A pang radiated through me at how well she had pegged Linus within minutes of meeting him. He would hate that. I was just teaching him to leave his masks in storage, and here was someone looking on his naked face and seeing more than he would ever want to share with a stranger. Maybe I was wrong to push him, but I couldn't shake the mental picture Barb had painted. It meshed too well with how I envisioned his *perfect* childhood.

The Grande Dame had raised him to be the High Society ideal. He was a prince among practitioners, a god among mortals. But he had been so lonely and so tired of the pretense. I owed it to him to open his eyes to the possibilities before he chose to leave them wide or screw them shut tight again.

"We're in the honeymoon suite." I redirected the conversation away from Linus. "You're welcome to any other room."

"We'll stay downstairs." She winked. "We'll give you newlyweds some privacy."

"We appreciate that." I checked with Linus, who was handing the phone back to Benny. "All settled?"

"Yes." Linus rejoined me. "Do you want to shower before dinner?"

"Let's." I hooked him by the collar then leaned around him to smile at Barb. "Make yourselves at home."

"We'll do that."

The shuffle of feet and murmur of voices relaxed my shoulders, banishing tension I hadn't noticed racking up since our arrival. Then it hit me. The problem. This house was wood and plaster and not much more. It lacked a soul. The quiet had been grating on my nerves, but I hadn't understood the root cause.

Fiddlesticks.

I was a grown woman on her honeymoon for pity's sake.

The last thing I ought to be was homesick.

Halfway up the stairs, I gagged on a pungent whiff of rotten eggs.

Magic peppered the air, but it moved in the opposite direction.

"Do you smell it?" Barb called from the base of the stairs. "That's how it always starts."

"Hard to miss." I covered my nose with the neck of my shirt, but it didn't help. "Goddess, that's rank."

"Just wait." Benny emerged, slung his arm around Barb's shoulders, and laughed. "It gets worse."

"We have photos from previous years if you'd like to see them," he offered. "They're in my cloud."

There it was, the offer I had hoped for, a lead on the mystery, but it couldn't have come at a worse time.

With two expectant vampires gazing up at us with starstruck excitement, I had no choice. "Sure."

The couple scattered, and I thumped my head against Linus's chest. "Whose idea was it to invite them in again?"

"I believe it was..." he trailed his cool fingers up my right side, the tips brushing my breast, "...yours."

"Linus," I moaned, leaning into him. "You're punishing me."

"Me?" His lips found mine, and my back hit the wall. "I would never."

Proving two could play his game, I slid my hand between us and relished his groan. "You were saying?"

"I apologize." His teeth found my neck and worried the delicate skin. "Profusely."

Knees liquifying as his hand covered my breast, his thumb teasing my nipple, I almost wet my pants when Barb yelled up at us, "We're ready."

"Be right there," I managed after my lungs remembered what to do with oxygen.

"Go shower." Linus dropped his hand. "I'll entertain them until you finish."

"Are you sure?" I had yet to drop mine. "*Really* sure?"

Eyelashes fluttering as I explored his length with my thumb, he rasped, "Yes."

Unable to resist nibbling on him too, I raked my teeth over the shell of his ear. "I love the way your breath catches when I—"

"Do you guys want any snacks?" Benny hollered. "There's popcorn and cookies in the kitchen."

"Tell you what, you take the first shower." I trailed my fingers up Linus's zipper and across his belt on my way past. "I've got a feeling you need one more than me."

A nice cold one.

SIX

Benny, Barb, and I gathered around the table in the dining room, and they vibrated with excitement. I ought to be happy they had proof of their relationship with the inn, but the groan of old pipes made it all too easy to focus on the shower happening upstairs...without me.

"We set up motion cameras in the halls last time." Benny pivoted his laptop toward me, and Barb mashed the play button, eager to share their findings. "We didn't catch much activity, but we did get this."

On the screen, a shadow split into two and then into four. The blurs prowled the hall like cats, their eyes bright in the darkness. Their target was clear. They aimed straight for the tripod, knocking its legs out from under it. One of them leaned in front of the camera and hissed a warning.

Chin on palm, Barb shook her head. "What do you think they are?"

"I have no idea." I watched again from the start. "They're bold. That's for sure."

"We have run-ins with them each time." Benny spun the

computer around, clicked a few times, then showed me another clip lined up for watching with a date sixty years earlier. "I can't decide if it's the same ones or not."

The scene played out the exact same way. A shadow appeared, it split into multiples, and it attacked the video equipment.

Thinking of Linus's wounds, I asked, "Have they ever hurt you?"

"A scratch here and there," Barb admitted, "but that's all."

"They were slow to heal." Benny showed me his arm. "This one stuck around."

Five thin lines marred his skin, all gone silver. More proof he was a young vampire. An older one would have healed the damage by now. Unless whatever toxin made Linus's healing complicated also held the power to affect the undead. Anything that potent would explain why his wounds hadn't wanted to close.

"We have more," Barb said. "Photos, I mean. That's the last of the video."

"I can sort through them," Linus said from the doorway. "Grier, it's your turn."

The vampires watched us like we were a nature special on the mating habits of necromancers.

"We got filthy earlier." I made a confession. "We were down in the basement."

"We figured." Benny chuckled. "We didn't want to say anything, but the smell…"

All that lovely shadow-cat feces. "Don't show him all the good stuff while I'm gone."

Getting to my feet, I turned to face Linus, and every train of thought in my brain station derailed.

He had come downstairs wearing a crisp white shirt undone with no undershirt to be found. His fingers moved over the buttons, but no progress appeared to be made. The result was I got an eyeful of tattooed skin damp from the shower.

I was not amused.

Crossing to my husband, I narrowed my eyes to slits. "This was cruel."

He knew how much I loved his body, what an eyeful of the gorgeous ink curving over the planes of his chest and abs did to me.

Leaning down, he brushed my ear with his lips. "This was payback."

"I'm a terrible influence on you."

"Yes," he agreed, his teeth catching my earlobe. "You are."

The Linus who first kissed me would have died from embarrassment before pulling shenanigans of this magnitude in front of an audience. Scratch that. The thought never would have entered his head. I would have done the instigating, and he would have flushed every Pantone shade of red. Years of PDA exposure therapy had worked wonders on him.

Though, seeing as how I was in desperate need of my own cold shower, I wasn't sure that was a good thing.

Working to keep my glower on, I sashayed past him into the hall. I made it halfway up the stairs before a goofy smile overtook me. I could get used to this. Being teased by Linus was almost as much fun as teasing him.

About to step onto the landing, I startled when a black smudge coalesced on the runner in front of me.

"Hi there." I kept my tone light. "Are you the little guy who likes to scratch people?"

The creature blinked yellow eyes then charged at full speed.

The twerp was trying to knock me down the stairs. "Not today."

Just before its paws hit my chest, I stepped down and over, giving it room to sail past.

Too bad a second one had been waiting behind me.

I stepped on it, yelped when it swatted my calf, then stepped up on instinct to escape. That might have worked if a third hadn't come to roost on the topmost step. It waited until all my weight balanced on the leg its shadowy friend was busy slicing and dicing then hit me square in the chest.

Arms windmilling, I couldn't regain my footing. There were too many of them, darting under my feet and throwing their weight against me in vicious pounces that left bloody pinpricks where they landed.

I couldn't help my scream as I fell, and I yanked on my bond with Cletus on instinct. He might not be corporeal enough to catch me, but he could slow me down, maybe keep me from breaking my neck. That would be nice. I would hate to go out on such a lame note. The obituary would be humiliating. After all I had survived, I would roll over in my grave if the Society papers reported this as my exit strategy.

Grier Woolworth, Potentate of Savannah, tripped over a shadow cat on the stairs and fell to her death.

As my life flashed before my eyes, I tumbled through a pocket of cold air with bony fingers that clawed at my shirt, my pants, my hair.

Cletus.

But I had built up too much momentum. He couldn't catch me. He didn't have that kind of strength.

Stick a fork in me, I was done.

A wall of cold muscle hit me from behind, and the air whooshed from my lungs. Tendrils of night spilled over my shoulder, and when I tipped my head back, I brushed the edge of Linus's tattered cowl with the top of my head.

"Hi," I gasped. "Fancy meeting you here."

Not one of my wittier one-liners, but Linus didn't smile. Neither did Cletus, who somehow ended up clutching my ankles.

"This was a bad idea." Linus hugged me close. "I shouldn't have brought you here."

"Oh, come on." I wriggled out of Cletus's grasp and got my feet back under me. "You can't call it quits after one itsy-bitsy attempted murder."

"This makes two."

"Ah." I lifted a finger. "But from two different sources."

Hrm. Yeah. In hindsight, I hadn't helped the situation by

reminding him of that. This was supposed to be a low-key haunting, but someone had cranked the dial as high as it would go.

"I wanted to indulge your interest in haunted history," he said, "not allow you to become a part of it."

"Oh dear." Barb rushed up the stairs to help, but Linus growled at her from the depths of his cloak. "Are you all right?"

"I'm good." I stood under my own steam, which didn't impress Linus much. "Those shadow cats are tiny bastards."

"That's what did this?" She slapped a hand over her heart. "Oh, dear. They're escalating then."

The vampires had the inside track on this haunting, so I took their word for it.

"Question." I leaned against the railing. "Has anyone or anything else ever attacked you here?"

"Goodness, no." She tugged on her necklace. "Just the cats." She eased closer. "What about you?"

With the library in smoky ruin and the wannabe arsonist at large, I didn't feel great about admitting our B&E had precipitated an explosion or that someone—possibly them—wanted us dead.

"No," I lied. "Just curious if there are any other surprises in store."

Barb's expression smoothed, but a stubborn line between her brows hinted she might not believe me. That suited me fine. It's not like I bought the yarn she was spinning either. Not all of it. There were too many frayed ends for me to pick at to trust their aw-shucks routine.

"I'm going to help Grier to our room," Linus clipped out in a firm tone. "We would prefer to remain undisturbed the rest of the evening."

"We're happy to trade if you decide you'd rather have ground-floor accommodations."

Aching from the knees down, I shot her a thumbs-up, but Linus didn't so much as blink in her direction.

Wisps of cold air licked my skin as he scooped me up into a bridal carry. Cletus circled us the whole climb, but the shadow cats had scattered after attacking me.

Linus didn't set me down until we entered our room, and he shut the door behind us, Cletus on guard detail in the hall.

"Can you stand?" He set me on my feet. "Did you hurt anything?"

"Ouch." I twisted my leg with effort to show him my calf. "They got me pretty good."

The blue in his eyes had long since darkened until black pools stared back at me. "Grier..."

"I'm not chickening out yet." I touched his cheek, his skin like ice. "Things are just starting to get good."

"Near-death experiences aren't what I would call good." He went for the button on my jeans, his fingers raising chills, but he kept his movements clinical. "We need to treat your wounds."

I helped as best I could, but the jeans were ruined, torn to ribbons and saturated with so much blood that it wouldn't be worth scrubbing out the stains. I almost told him to toss them, but I could turn them into cutoffs. Maybe. And bleach them.

Gah.

The curse of being cheap—I mean, *frugal.*

"How do you want me?" I eyed the bed, but I was still gross. "Do we have another comforter?"

"No." He did the same math as me, paused to draw a sigil on the doorframe, then entered the bathroom and started the hot water for a shower. "Do you think you can stand long enough to get clean?"

A tub would have been more welcome, but I didn't want to soak in shadow cat-poop stew.

"I'll make it happen." I limped to him. "I don't want to risk contamination on top of the toxin."

A sigil could seal the wounds, sure, but that didn't mean it purged them. Magic acted weird on me on a good day. Already I was experiencing pain where Linus hadn't felt a thing. *Better safe than sorry* when mixing magic with a goddess-touched necromancer had become our golden rule.

Linus, ever the gentleman, stripped down to his boxers and stepped into the shower with me.

"You could have taken those off." I was all too happy to slump against him. "We *are* married now."

"You're hurt, and I'm not allowing distractions."

Hooking his arm around my waist, he held me upright to keep pressure off my calves while I washed my hair and upper body. Then came the fun part. I wasn't sure how I would manage until he scooped me up—again—and sat me on the floor of the stall. He knelt in front of me, water tugging his hair into his eyes, and began to slowly clean and examine every mark.

"You're staring," he murmured, his fingers light and careful.

"I can do that." I tapped the ring on his finger. "You're all mine." I flicked bubbles at him. "Mine, mine, mine."

"You sound like Lethe when she sings her donut song." Scraping the dark auburn curtain away from his face, he smiled at me with so much love and surprise and hope it physically hurt. "Am I your donut?"

"Don't put ideas in my head." I pouted. "You've already said no funny business."

"You're bleeding."

"Not much."

"Enough."

"I've got plenty more where that came from."

Linus shook his head. "You're going to be the death of me."

"Nah." I touched his cool cheek. "I like you too much."

"Come on." He lifted me, carried me out, and bundled me in towels until I was the envy of every well-dressed mummy. He forgot to turn off the water, which made me smile. He had grown used to Woolly helping us out too. "Don't move."

"I wouldn't…" I wet my lips when he dropped his soggy under-wear. "Oh."

"I mean it." He wrapped the last towel around his hips. "I'm going to get my kit."

"You never let me have any fun," I pouted when Linus returned fully dressed. "You could have at least played doctor with me naked."

"I'm not that strong." His grip tightened on the knot. "Resisting you is hard enough as it is."

"You say the sweetest things." I cuddled against him, drenching his shirt. "You make it sound like you could Hulk out and ravage me at any moment."

When Linus turned his gaze on me and his eyes were black from corner to corner, I couldn't help my smile. You might say that unraveling his self-control had become a hobby of mine, one I practiced often.

"I'll behave." I crossed a finger over my heart. "Promise."

His gaze dipped, black tendrils unfurling around him, and he growled low in his throat.

"Sorry," I whispered, folding my hands primly in my lap. "I really will behave."

Linus sat me at the foot of the bed then helped me turn onto my stomach and stretch out my legs.

"I'm going to try closing these with a healing sigil," he murmured, his voice rough. "We'll go from there."

The magic took the sting out of the wounds, but it didn't accomplish much else. I hadn't expected it to, given how Linus had reacted, but it was worth a shot.

Testing his patch job, I gave an experimental flex that set my leg on fire. "Want me to give it a try?"

He raked a calculating glance the length of my thigh. "Can you reach?"

"Good question."

I would have offered to give him my blood and let him do it, but goddess-touched magic worked only for goddess-touched necromancers, as far as I could tell. That didn't make it any safer for my blood to fall into enemy hands. There was always someone clever, ambitious, or desperate enough to figure out a workaround for most anything.

With effort, I got myself sitting on the foot of the mattress, back where we started. "Knife?"

Linus passed me my pocketknife and hovered as if unsure how best to help.

The combination of our stress must have summoned Cletus, who arrived with a downcast head and linked hands. He looked… guilty. Even his moan of inquiry came out higher and tighter than usual.

The sight of my blood on the bedspread wasn't doing Linus's blood pressure any favors, so I let the wraith off the hook for the moment and focused on how best to position myself with minimal ouchiness. In the end, there was no way to avoid more pain as I crossed one leg, bracing that ankle over my knee.

The quick bite of my blade drew blood, and I used it as ink to draw on the healing sigil that had worked on Linus. Magic filled my hands, and I sank it into the furrows, leaving my skin glowing and my pores sparkling.

"Your palm." Linus caught it in his. "You're still bleeding."

"The sigil didn't work on my calves, either." I uncrossed my legs. "Ow."

"Lie down." He rifled through his kit. "We'll have to do this the old-fashioned way."

"Goody." Used to the drill, I spread out again. "I wonder what's up with my hand."

"The toxin might have an anticoagulant in it. It could be stopping your blood from clotting."

"Ugh." I held out my hand to him since it was making the bigger mess, and he cleaned it, smeared his own antibacterial concoction on it, then bandaged it up tight. "The claw marks didn't bleed this much."

"You cut hard when you're healing." He pressed his lips to the bandage, kissing my boo-boo. "The scratches aren't as deep."

"They feel like it," I grumbled. "They sting like you're pouring peroxide on them."

"I am pouring peroxide on them."

"Oh." I glanced over my shoulder at him. "Well that explains it then." His soft huff of laughter told me we were over the hump. "You want to watch a movie and make out when you're done?"

"Yes and no." He gave me a stern glance that held too much heat and amusement to sting. "You're going to rest and heal. We can make out tomorrow, if you're a good girl."

"Sex has really changed you." I sighed dramatically. "I remember the days when you were innocent…"

Heat crept up his throat. "You have only yourself to blame."

"True." I had trouble containing my smile. "I will gladly take the credit for corrupting you."

The wraith touched my shoulder, moaned unintelligible words, and left us alone.

"He's acting weird." I drummed my fingers on the mattress. "Do you think he's okay?"

"Cletus is a singularity, so it's hard to say." He finished cleaning and medicating my calves then wrapped them with bandages. "Most likely, he's worried about you or still upset about your fall."

"Hmm."

When Linus finished, he helped me turn over and propped me against the headboard. "Are you hungry?"

"Use your best judgment."

"That's a yes."

"Yes, that is a yes."

"Do you need anything else from the kitchen?" He made zero progress toward the door. "I'm going to lock you in from the hall while I'm gone so you don't have to get up again."

"I wouldn't say no to a bottle of water." I flexed my toes, which didn't help with the itching under my bandages. At all. "My throat feels like I swallowed all the dust in the basement."

He left, eventually, but he didn't look happy about it.

Since I had time on my hands, I checked my email. I had a message from Bishop but decided to wait on Linus to read it. With that decision made, I dialed up my bestie to see what trouble she had been getting into without me. "Hiya."

"Hi yourself." A *tick, tick, tick* filled the background. "Your honeymoon was a total bust, huh? Must be if you're calling me twenty-four hours in instead of making sweet, sweet love to your hubby."

"There was an accident," I confessed. "Sweet, sweet love has been put on hold."

"What kind of accident?" A growl entered her voice. "Do I have to eat someone?"

The temptation to make a cat and dog joke was there, but I managed to swallow it with minimal choking. "How much do you know about our honeymoon plans?"

"Everything." She scoffed. "Do you really think we'd let you out of our sight otherwise?"

"I haven't been kidnapped in years, and no one hardly ever tries to murder me anymore."

"Until tonight."

"Okay, fine. Until tonight."

And the night before, but who was counting?

A masculine voice murmured what sounded like directions, and brakes squealed in my ear. "Are you and Hood going somewhere?"

"You could say that." She hissed at him to be quiet. "Don't worry about us."

Call me crazy, but I didn't like the tone of this call. "How's Keet?"

"He's been watching an anime series about a dragon egg or a dragon prince with our little diva." The ticking noise resumed then switched off. "He tried to incubate the boiled egg from her breakfast, so we gave him an Easter egg from last year, one of the tiny decorative ones. He's been sitting on it ever since."

"As long as he's happy?" I exhaled. "Let's cross our fingers they run out of episodes before he realizes his egg will never hatch. Switch to *The Lion King* if he starts getting depressed about it. Nothing cheers him up like making farting warthog noises."

"Yeah, yeah." Tires screeched, and Hood swore, but Lethe's breath didn't so much as catch. "I know the drill."

The call ended without another word, and I pulled back to look at my phone. Almost immediately, it rang, and I answered, "Hello again."

"Sorry about that," Hood apologized. "Eva connected her cell phone to our radio, and we can't figure out how to override hers with ours, so it keeps dropping calls."

Ah, the joys of parenthood and having a tech-savvy kid. "I totally understand."

We made goodbye noises, and I flopped back in bed to wait on Linus.

I was halfway to dozing when a mournful baying raised the hairs down my arms.

"There's no way." I slid off the bed and hobbled to the window. "She wouldn't..."

The noise didn't come again, and I started doubting whether I had heard it in the first place. Probably wishful thinking. Our situation was getting more intense, and backup wouldn't be the worst idea ever, not that I would admit it to Cletus. I was no longer sure we could solve this haunting within our time limit, but the potentate in me felt obligated to try.

The door swung open before I reached the bed.

Busted.

"What are you doing up?" Linus entered with a tray he must have found downstairs in his hands. "Did you see something outside?"

"I heard something." I tottered in his direction. "I probably imagined it."

Noticing the phone on the quilt, he asked, "Any news?"

"Bishop touched base with me." I sat on the mattress and pulled up the message. "No families of any shape or size have gone missing in a fifty-mile radius during the last thirty days, so that's a break in the pattern."

"Or it hasn't been reported yet." He joined me. "If they were traveling or on vacation, it might take time for their family and friends to realize something is wrong."

"True." I set my cell aside. "I was hoping for a neon sign or flashing lights or something."

"Sadly, villains tend not to advertise their dastardly deeds until after they've been successfully committed."

"And yet, I haven't given up hope of it happening one day, preferably on a high-profile case without any other leads to follow. Then bam! A glowing arrow pointing to the bad guy."

Handing over a bowl of his famously buttery popcorn plus a box of Raisinets and Junior Mints, he tucked me against him. "We can dream."

We settled down to watch a movie with our most excellent snacks, and I filled him in on my odd call with Lethe while we snuggled. Linus slept on top of the covers with his clothes on. That is to say he made himself comfortable and resumed adding notes to a book he was writing on the goddess-touched condition meant for me and any future goddess-touched necromancers in the family.

I drifted to sleep listening to the scratch of his pen across paper and the soothing coolness of his skin next to mine.

<h1 style="text-align:center">SEVEN</h1>

Linus sat in bed next to Grier and stared at the paragraph he wrote an hour ago. The more times he read over it, the less sense it made. His concentration was shot, so he set aside his work and sucked in a long, calming breath.

The howl of dark magics in his blood demanded satisfaction for Grier's injuries, and he was tempted to give himself over to that power. But that's not who he was, and he reined in the familiar impulse with effort that broke sweat across his brow.

He had put off leaving Grier for as long as he dared, but he had business to attend before she rose at dusk. Careful not to wake her, he eased out of bed and exited the room, locking her in before he confronted the guilty wraith.

Fading as the sun rose, Cletus bobbed on unfelt air currents, and Linus waited for him to confess.

"You might as well tell me what you've done." Linus searched the hall and the stairs, but he found nothing amiss on his way to the foyer. "I'm about to find out whether you own up to it or not."

Stubborn to a fault, a new personality quirk that reminded him painfully of Maud, the wraith kept his silence.

The vampires were nowhere in sight, and Linus sighed with relief. He didn't mind sharing the house. He would never tell Grier he preferred more victims to shift the target off her back, but she knew him well enough to guess he wouldn't turn down anyone who could defend themselves if they asked for a room.

"I know you're out here," Linus called from the porch after shutting the front door behind him. "The question is why."

Dark figures loped into view, two large dogs covered in rough scales, their tongues lolling.

When he turned to address Cletus, the wraith was nowhere to be found and refused to answer a summons.

The smaller beast transformed in a swirl of crimson magic into a compact woman with bright-blue hair.

"Cletus appeared to us." She jogged up the steps and joined him. "He moaned what I interpreted as Grier being in danger." Lethe spread her hands in a helpless gesture. "So here we are."

Grier's relationship with Lethe, Hood, and their pack was best described as...complicated.

Lethe was her best friend, but Grier was also Lethe's daughter's godmother. Even if those two things hadn't been the case, Grier was also a member of the Savannah gwyllgi pack by virtue of a debt Hood and Lethe felt was owed to her on her mother's behalf.

A magically enforced NDA the alpha pair signed prevented them from sharing the details, but it had been made clear to us that their failure to protect Grier's mother had created an imbalance, in their minds, in need of rectifying.

Technically, after the wedding, Linus had joined the pack as well. All that added up to a lot of red tape he thought he had already cut through in order to escape with Grier for a handful of days.

"I told her we should call first," Hood said after his own transformation. "She refused on the basis that Grier is—"

"—my best friend." Lethe elbowed him in the side, and he bent over coughing.

"Yeah," Hood wheezed, glaring at her. "That."

As social intricacies often eluded him, Linus felt no shame in asking, "Am I missing something?"

Hood looked anywhere but at him while Lethe widened her eyes in a failed attempt at innocence.

"You might as well join us." Linus gestured toward the inn. "A vampire couple showed up last night and requested a room. What are two more guests?"

Lethe bristled, her lip twitching with the promise of a growl. "Anything we should worry about?"

Usually, Linus respected her heightened overprotective streak where her packmates were concerned. Even umbrella members such as Grier and himself. Tonight, he selfishly regretted it. Just a bit.

"I don't think so." He hesitated. "They claim they're here because of the haunting."

A neat line knitted her brow. "Okay, that's weird."

As undead creatures, vampires preferred to surround themselves with life, not death.

"They have evidence that supports their story."

Lethe wasn't letting go. "What kind?"

"Video and photos from the house during previous years."

"Have you spoken to the owners?" Hood stared off in the direction of a small cottage set behind the main house. "Someone had to check them in, right?"

"They self-checked, but I spoke to Mr. Oliphant first. He wanted to make certain we didn't mind the intrusion." He thought back on the conversation, but their host had been courteous to a fault, the same as he had been at their own check-in. "The Rogoffs claim to be regular patrons, but he didn't recognize their names. That's to be expected. It's not as if they could use the same identity each time without drawing suspicion."

An inn this small, in a town so remote, with a history so dark, could use all the business it could get. It could be the owners didn't mind who filled the rooms as long as they got paid. Shortsighted if this event was a draw for regular customers, since he and Grier wouldn't be coming back, but it was hard to turn down the promise of a rather large payday, regardless of what future complications their present actions set in motion.

"Let's give it a few hours." Hood flared his nostrils. "Then I think we should go talk to them."

"Not all vampires are murderous fiends," Linus said dryly. "Most are perfectly average."

"I'm not saying the whole species is a wash," Lethe countered, arms crossed, "but even you have to admit they tend to kidnap first and ask questions never around Grier."

Forced to agree with her, Linus summoned Cletus. "Go check on the Oliphants."

The wraith shimmered, a faint smudge, then vanished again, off to fulfil its duty.

"Are you going to tell Grier we're here?" Lethe scuffed her boot in the grass. "I don't want her to think I'm a codependent psycho who can't deal with her best friend leaving for a few days."

The lack of eye contact made him curious. "How *did* you get here so fast?"

Savannah was an eight-hour drive or about a four-hour flight, counting the unavoidable layover, if they left from Atlanta. The incident with Grier on the stairs happened only a few hours earlier. Cletus could appear to Lethe and Hood to convey his message in an instant, but they couldn't traverse space in a blink the same way.

"She's a codependent psycho who can't deal with her best friend leaving for a few days." Hood wiped the smile off his face with his hand, but his eyes still grinned. "We were already on our way when the wraith popped in to say hello."

Lethe and Grier were as close as sisters, but Lethe wasn't usually this clingy. "Any particular reason why you're worried about Grier?"

Lethe scrunched up her face, working through her options, which didn't bode well, when Cletus shot a warning jolt down the bond he shared with Linus. The connection was instinctual after so many years together, and he peered through the wraith's eyes to view the issue.

"We have a problem." He spared one last glance toward the inn before an ingrained sense of duty from his tenure as the Potentate of Atlanta urged him toward the cottage. Vision flickering between his own and Cletus's, he picked his way across the unfamiliar landscape. "We need to go to the Oliphants."

The gwyllgi followed him, but they hung back when they reached the cottage.

"I smell it." Lethe rubbed at her nose. "This is not going to be a social call."

Again, he found himself staring after the inn. And again, he forced his thoughts back on task.

"There are bodies in there," Hood confirmed. "Fresh ones."

"The Oliphants." Linus had already viewed the brutal tableau secondhand. "They're both dead."

Kylie was around the same age as Grier was when she stumbled across Maud in a pool of blood gone cold. Linus regretted that security had been ripped away from them both so young, but this time he could ward the cottage and spare Kylie from the nightmares Grier still carried with her. It wasn't much, but it was the best he could do. That, and find the person or persons responsible.

A hazy dawn broke before he could order Cletus back to Grier. With the vampires asleep for the day, and the shadow cats banished until nightfall, she would be safe behind the sigil on her door. He had the time before she woke to begin working toward justice for the Oliphants.

"The door is locked." Falling into old habits, he began his investigation. "Windows are too." He circled the cottage, checking all entry points until he reached the back door. "There are signs this lock was jimmied." He examined it more closely. "The wood has weathered beneath the damage. That means it's old." He straightened. "This was not how the killers gained access."

"Agree," the gwyllgi chimed in.

Consulting with the alpha pair, he gave them room to work. "Are you picking up any unusual scents?"

"Human and vampire." Hood checked with Lethe. "The human ones are layered, a product of time. They belonged to the residents. The vampires are new and recent."

A gnawing suspicion blossomed in his gut. "There are more than one?"

"A pair," Lethe confirmed. "Male and female."

"There's overlap within them too," Hood added. "I'm guessing a mated couple."

Another thought occurred to him. "Any traces of accelerant?"

"See those red metal cans? Gasoline." Lethe pointed to an ancient lawnmower parked under a weather-beaten awning extending off the rear of the house. "There's a splash of diesel too, but that might be from a vehicle."

"Why do you ask?" Hood poked around, but he circled back with a shrug. "What am I missing?"

The weight of Lethe's stare fell on Linus, and he grasped too late that Grier hadn't told her everything.

Pinching the bridge of his nose, he told them about the trip to the library and the visit from the arsonist.

"Ha." Lethe stabbed Hood in the chest. "I told you Grier needed us."

Once Lethe finished being smug, which took a while, they returned to the front of the cottage.

"The vampires walked right onto the porch." Hood flared his nostrils. "They didn't touch the knob or the door, but they used the railing. They must have been let in before they could knock."

"The Oliphants have been innkeepers for generations. It's likely they would have welcomed prospective guests into their home." Linus thought back on his phone conversation with Mr. Oliphant, which gave an approximate time of death. "The Rogoffs must have called to book a room, learned the inn was full, then came here for information on who was occupying the house."

"Pros," Hood murmured. "They wanted to tailor their cover story to fit whoever they encountered."

And they had settled on the lovey-dovey couple act to con a pair of honeymooners since they were a mated pair.

"Are we going in?" Lethe squared her shoulders. "You can pop the lock, right?"

"Yes." He did so with a sigil drawn using his pen. "Disturb as little as possible." He hesitated with a hand on the knob and met their eyes. "I'll have to call the cleaners, but not yet. I would prefer to avoid a reprimand for contaminating evidence, so let's make this quick."

Activity on that scale at the cottage would draw the vampires' attention, and Linus didn't want them to bolt until he divined their true purpose in coming here. Justice for the Oliphants was beyond the reach of human law now, but the murderers were still within his grasp.

Once Linus confirmed these were vampire kills, the cleaners would take over, coordinating with local law enforcement after they had collected their evidence. Then they would dispose of the bodies and all signs of supernatural involvement.

The lock twisted with a grating metallic shift, and Linus opened the door. As he did so, a black cat prowled out and stropped his leg with a purr. Upon noticing Lethe and Hood, it hissed, fur bristling, and vanished into the night.

"I hope that wasn't the family pet," Lethe murmured then added on a hopeful note. "Maybe it's allowed outside?"

Concerns for the cat vanished when the scent hit Linus, and he started breathing through his mouth.

Entering the house, he located the bodies, coughing when the sour, meaty tang hit the back of his throat. The wife had died first, by her own hand. A knitting needle protruded from the side of her neck, and her fingers were soaked with blood that had poured down her shoulder to ruin her clothes and the chair where she sat. Her expression was oddly peaceful. Her husband, on the other hand, died with his face contorted, the fingers of one hand broken, the digits twisted out of shape.

"The wife committed suicide." Hood knelt beside her. "The vampires didn't lay a finger on her."

"They tortured the husband," Lethe growled. "What could two little old people have known that was worth this?"

The average person would break long before their second finger, but they had worked over Mr. Oliphant. He had held on until they got what they wanted and they killed him, or else they ran out of time to extract the information because he died from his injuries. What had been worth their lives to protect?

"Look how they ripped out his throat." Hood kept his tone level. "That speaks of temper."

"He was out here, alone with the body of his wife, while I was talking to him on the phone." Linus's temper crackled, and the noise in his head, the darkness, howled. "The vampires must have circled back to finish this after I carried Grier up to our room."

"If he was out here alone, then they were certain he would play his part. They must have glamoured him out of his mind." Hood eyed the man with pity. "He couldn't have asked for help even if he realized he needed it. The glamour wouldn't allow it."

"This isn't your fault." Lethe jutted out her chin. "Fight me."

"What she means," Hood said, clasping him on the shoulder, "is that what happened to the Oliphants is part of what's been happening here for generations. You didn't set these events in motion."

"That's what I said," Lethe protested. "It's not his fault."

Hood rubbed his face then let his hands fall to his sides before sighing, "Yes, dear."

The gwyllgi bantering only worked so long before Linus could no longer ignore the gruesome scene.

As regret burned in his gut, he turned away from the Oliphants.

The vampires hadn't fed on them. They had let their blood waste.

There was an insult in that, not only in the taking of a life but the squandering of a life once taken.

"Mr. Oliphant didn't give it up, whatever it was," Lethe said, drawing Linus from his grim thoughts. "Otherwise, I don't see the vampires inviting themselves to the inn knowing you and Grier were there." Lethe prowled around the space. "They must still be searching for whatever brought them here."

Linus drifted through each room, searching without making it obvious so the cleaners could do their jobs with minimal interference later. The house was neat, everything in its place, and the decor dated back to the sixties. Even the crucifixes on the walls, and there were dozens, came in the popular turquoise shade of the appliances from that era. So did the frames for all the paintings of saints.

He located the source of the Rogoffs' elaborate costumes in the master closet. Apparently square dancing was a hobby the Oliphants had enjoyed together. The Rogoffs must have stolen the clothes to fit their story about traveling for a competition. With the couple dead, there was no one to expose them for the theft. Except for Kylie.

On the kitchen table, he spied three sagging boxes with their yellowed lids tossed aside. He dug through their contents and exhaled with self-directed annoyance at the damning evidence they contained.

One sat empty. Another held tapes from previous years, the full twenty-four-hour cycle, clearly marked with the date. The final held photos ranging from digital crispness to fading Polaroid to black-and-white stills. The handwriting on the back matched the photos Linus had flipped through with the Rogoffs earlier. The vampires must have emptied a box of its contents before concocting their cover story.

"There's a fifth scent here that doesn't belong to the couple or to the vampires." Hood brought a report card pinned on the fridge to his nose. "It's heavy on male hormones."

"They have a grandson who self-identifies as a granddaughter. Her name is Kylie." Linus raked his fingers through his hair. "She's been staying in the subbasement, a level above the maze."

"Are you kidding me?" Lethe slid into mothering mode. "Who in their right mind would let her do that?"

"She claimed things weren't great at home." Linus led them to her room. "This doesn't support that."

The walls had been painted lavender, and a fuzzy pink area rug covered the hardwood floor. Her sheets were soft blue, and her comforter was white eyelet lace with extra frills along the edges. Trophies for JV soccer and football blended with more recent ones for varsity cheerleading. A peek in the closet revealed a rainbow of coordinating outfits with shoes to match, all name brand.

"Competition at this level costs." Linus indicated the gold all-state medal from this year hung over a lamp near the bed. "Both time and money."

"The grandparents were definitely funding the dream." Lethe had located a baby-pink photo album with *It's a Girl* embossed on the cover. "Look at this."

Page after page illustrated how much they loved her. Hugging after a football game, grinning from ear to ear at dinner, tearing up when she placed in competitions. These people had supported her choices. Including her recent change of pronoun. So why had Kylie lied about her homelife? From what he could tell, her mother and father weren't in the picture. They certainly weren't in any photos. Only her grandparents had been present.

"She just happened to spend the night at the inn when vamps showed up and slaughtered her family?" Hood scratched his cheek. "It doesn't vibe for me."

"There's more to this," Lethe agreed. "The grandparents must have expected trouble and sent her away."

"Grier and I discovered Kylie prior to the vampires' arrival." Linus returned to the kitchen. "She laughed off a fall down the stairs." His gaze snagged on the empty box and lingered. "She gave us no indication she was afraid for herself or her grandparents."

But she hadn't exactly been upfront with them either. He wasn't certain how much of what she had told them was the truth and how much was what she thought they wanted to hear.

"They might have relocated her as a preventative measure," Hood said. "But why send her to the inn?"

"You'd think it would be a last resort," Lethe agreed. "What with the haunting and all."

"Unless they had reason to know she would be safe there," Hood offered. "The family hasn't been targeted, right?"

Linus shook his head, but his thoughts spun toward the nest the girl had made for herself.

"I don't see them ushering her into danger. It's clear her grandparents loved her very much. They must have believed it was best for her." Lethe intruded on his thoughts. "I could see her grandfather taking a lot of hurt to keep her, and her location, safe." She shrugged. "It's what parents do."

Without any traces of her mother or father, that's what the Oliphants would have been to her: parents.

"We'll wait until the sun is fully up, and then we'll go down after her." Linus glanced out the window at the purple and pink sky. "We need to secure her before the vampires do to her what they did to her grandparents."

Old vampires could move around during the day as long as they stayed indoors, but most succumbed to sleep and weren't easily awakened after sunrise. Without knowing the Rogoffs' ages, they had no way to gauge their strengths.

"For what it's worth," Hood added, "I don't scent any gasoline or diesel in the house."

The presence of the cans wasn't enough to implicate them any more than the absence of its scent in the home exonerated them.

"I should get back." Linus guided them from the cottage. "I don't want to leave Grier alone for long."

"That's probably for the best." Lethe gnawed her bottom lip. "We'll patrol the grounds."

After he sealed the door with a sigil, he took their measure. "Are you sure you don't want to come in?"

"Grier will figure it out," Hood warned, his tone sharp. "Now might be a good time to be forthcoming."

Teeth bared, Lethe growled at him. "Hush your face."

Hood rolled his eyes and shoved his hands into his pockets.

If Grier were here, she would wade in and demand to know the cause of the friction between them, but Linus wasn't used to finagling secrets from people without the liberal application of bribes.

"I'm not certain," Linus added for all the good it would do, "but I think she heard one of you a few hours ago."

"Damn that rabbit and its deliciousness," Lethe grumbled. "I didn't mean to whip out the hunting song, but that white tail flashed me, and it was over."

About to part ways, Linus noticed movement on the upper floor of the inn and lifted a hand in greeting.

"Uh-oh." Lethe followed his line of sight to where Grier stood framed in the window. "Busted."

Hood didn't say a word, but his mocking smile as they filed into the inn spoke volumes.

EIGHT

oing forward, the buddy system was in full effect whenever we used the stairs. Even if I had wanted to meet the guilty trio in the foyer, I couldn't get out of the room without Linus to erase the sigil on the door. With that in mind, I was left glowering through the window as they trudged to the porch with their chins tucked. Only when they were out of sight did I sit on the mattress to wait.

The sun was up, so Cletus was gone. Otherwise, I would have shaken him until answers fell out of his cloak.

This whole trip was fast becoming ridiculous.

The knob twisted as Linus released the ward on the room, and it annoyed me all over again to have been locked in and left out of the loop.

"Surprise!" Lethe bounded in, all smiles. "Miss me?"

Hood remained in the hall like he was scared I might explode and he wanted to stay clear of the blast.

Lethe and Hood's arrival must have come as a surprise to Linus too. He wasn't in the habit of keeping secrets from me, and this qualified as a whopper. Probably why he braved the room and crossed to me while the others hesitated. He sat on the bed and took my hand, and I read the exhaustion on his features.

"What's happened?" I linked our fingers. "Why are Hood and Lethe here?"

"The Oliphants were murdered." Linus brought our joined hands to his mouth and pressed a kiss to the knuckle above my wedding band. "Hood and Lethe need to cross-reference the Rogoffs' scents to be certain, but I can't imagine another pair of vampires are responsible."

"Goddess," I breathed. "What about Kylie?"

"She wasn't home," he said, and I heard what he wasn't saying.

For her to have avoided the same fate, her grandparents must have had an inkling of what was coming and sent her away.

Suddenly, her subbasement digs made a lot more sense, and trouble at home took on all new meaning.

"We need to find her." I read the same thoughts on his face. "She'll be safe while the sun is up, but we need her secure come nightfall."

"I'll find her," he promised. "I'll start the search once you're settled in for the day."

The poor kid had hard news coming her way, and I wished there was someone else to deliver it. Having lost my mother and adoptive mother to violent ends, I felt kinship with Kylie over her loss. That didn't mean I wanted to revisit my own pain through hers.

Years later, it still hurt too much. Maybe it made me a coward, but I was glad when Linus didn't invite me to come along.

The news, however grim, didn't explain the elephant—or should I say gwyllgi?—in the room. "How did Hood and Lethe get here so fast?"

The Oliphants couldn't have been dead long. Linus had spoken to Mr. Oliphant shortly after the Rogoffs appeared on our doorstep. I wasn't great with math, but Savannah wasn't exactly a hop, skip, and a jump away. I was missing something.

"Cletus warned us you were in danger." Lethe rocked her weight from front to back. "How could we not come?"

"Mm-hmm." I stared at her until she squished up her face. "I wasn't injured that long ago."

"Fine." She threw up her hands. "I was worried about you, okay? I didn't plan on you knowing we were here." She muttered about a damn tasty rabbit under her breath. "I figured Hood and I would patrol the property until the anniversary thing passed then beat you home."

"You're so codependent." I opened my arms and waited for her to fly into them. "Thank you."

"I really didn't mean to interrupt your couples' time." She hugged me, but not hard. It was odd, her embracing me and me still being able to breathe. She must be worried I got hurt worse than I had admitted after my fall. "I brought donuts, but I ate them all."

"That's okay." I waved off her apology. "I'm ready for bed and too sleepy to brush my teeth again."

With a sage nod, she intoned, "I admire your dedication to oral hygiene."

"Pick a room, any room." I flicked my wrist. "You might as well stay in the murder house since you're here."

"Murder house?" Her gaze shot to Linus. "I thought only light scratching was involved."

"Turns out a severed head was found on the property."

"I told him saving the research for the trip was a dumb idea." She smacked her forehead with her palm. "I told him, but did he listen? No. And now it's definitely a murder house."

"Murder house adjacent." I glared a warning for her to knock off the *I told you so* crap before Linus beat himself up worse over his decision to bring us here. "Besides, half the fun is solving the mystery. If he already knew who done it, what would have been the point in coming?"

"Lethe," Hood said, a gentle reprimand.

She deflated a little, gnawed on her lip, then shook her head once.

"I'm going down to fetch Kylie." Linus bent to kiss my forehead then slung his kit over his shoulder. "We need to put her somewhere safe where the vampires can't find her."

"I'll go with you," Hood volunteered. "Grier, would you mind catching Lethe up to speed?"

"You're not half bad at making me feel useful while also keeping me confined to my bed," I admitted. "I'm impressed."

"I do what I can." He kissed Lethe then nudged her toward me with a significant look. "You girls talk."

Lethe sprung onto the bed and made herself at home on Linus's side.

Once the boys left, I shifted toward her. "What was that all about?"

Rather than answer, she mirrored my pose. "Can I tell you after the honeymoon?"

That did not sound like she was sitting on good news. "*Will* you tell me after the honeymoon?"

"Yes." She laughed. "I just want you to have fun—"

"—while I still can?" I finished for her. "That's not ominous at all."

Lethe was like a dog with a bone when she wanted to be, and I was too tired to play tug-of-war. I would let her keep her secrets until dusk. Then I would lean on her or have Linus bribe her with bacon hot from the pan, until she made her confession.

"Go to sleep, Grier." She gave me a playful nudge that rolled me onto my back. "We've got ghosts to bust tonight, and you want to look your best."

"You're a nut bar."

"But I'm your nut bar."

Softly, I laughed myself to sleep.

NINE

The stairs creaked and moaned underfoot as Linus descended into the foyer with Hood, after the gwyllgi confirmed that Kylie wasn't upstairs. He hated to admit the noises made him miss Woolworth House that much more. He had always loved the old house, but she was truly his home now. She was the heart of the ever-expanding family Grier was gathering around them, and everywhere else felt soulless and empty in comparison.

"I smell them." Hood directed himself to the Rogoffs' suite when they hit the foyer. "They're in there."

"Good." Linus drew a sigil on their door, locking them in until he released them. "Kylie?"

"Her scent crisscrosses this floor, but it's hours old." He frowned. "She must have hit every single room."

"She might have changed her hiding place more often to lessen the odds of us finding her."

"Maybe," Hood agreed, but he didn't sound convinced. "Let's double-check to be sure."

With Hood's nose leading the way, they eliminated the prime

hiding spots in record time. He was right. Kylie had opened every door and drawer in the downstairs. Her scent marked every quilt, every light switch, and every knob. As if she was searching for something.

"There's a funky smell in here." Hood tracked the freshest trail to the pantry. "Rotten eggs."

"It gets worse." Linus opened the basement door then fished out his modified pen. "Do you mind?"

"Not at all." Hood didn't move a muscle. "Do your worst."

That unwavering trust left Linus's palms damp. His reputation was such that not many would allow him carte blanche without an angle. To have a friend extend that faith as easy as breathing...it humbled him.

"This is one of Grier's creations." He drew the light sigil on Hood's left palm. "It will come in handy in the basement."

"Handy." He chuckled. "I see what you did there."

The joking felt good too. Hood treated him the same whether or not Grier was around, so he wasn't trying to earn points with his wife's best friend by palling around with her husband or simply indulging a valuable ally. It made Linus grateful all over again for having Grier, and everything that came with her, in his life.

After giving his own palm the same treatment, Linus popped the lock and led them down the stairs into the basement. He stood back and gave Hood room to search it from corner to corner, but he showed no interest beyond the partially concealed door.

"Let me guess." He snorted. "That's our way in."

The rhetorical question, Linus ignored. "Can you tell if anyone is home?"

"The cocktail of teenage hormones and fear is pungent, but so is the feces and urine." He shot Linus a questioning glance. "What the hell is down there anyway?"

"Grier calls them shadow cats."

"The creatures who attacked her on the stairs?"

"The very same."

"This ought to be good." He dropped to his knees. "Here, kitty, kitty."

He shoved the door wide then shimmied into the opening headfirst.

Linus followed, a smile in place.

"This is the first level." He took the lead while Hood examined the hall. "Kylie is one down."

"How hard did you have to look to find this inn?" Hood whistled. "What a freak show."

"Not hard," Linus admitted. "Vetting it was more difficult."

With his connections within the paranormal community, it was a simple matter to locate a haunted inn. Validating its spiritual activity was much harder, and it required him to send in a proxy to get a feel for it.

"I bet." Hood touched the nearest wall, and splinters flaked off on his palm. "This place is all wood?"

"With the exception of the exterior foundation, yes."

"No offense to Mr. Oliphant," he said, dusting his hands, "but his architect was whackadoodle."

Based on what he had seen the of the subbasements so far, Linus was inclined to agree.

"Can I ask you a question?" He led the way to the trapdoor, keeping his back to Hood in case he declined. "A personal one."

"Shoot."

Surprised to find himself pushing the issue, he still managed to get out the question. "Why have things been tense between you and Lethe since you arrived?"

"She knows a secret." Hood exhaled long and hard. "I think she should tell. She disagrees."

There was little doubt who the secret involved. "Should I be concerned?"

"I swore not to spill the beans until after the honeymoon." He chuckled like he couldn't believe she had extracted the promise from him. "I have to keep my word. You understand, right?" His laughter deepened. "Now that you're a married man, you get that ain't nobody happy unless the mate is happy."

The push and pull of wanting to demand more information while respecting his friend's boundaries left Linus torn in a way he wasn't sure he ever had been. Ultimately, Lethe and Hood were here to protect Grier. If either of them had pertinent information, they would share it.

"I trust you," Linus said, and the weight of it made Hood pause and then grin.

"We're family." He slugged Linus in the shoulder. "Who else are you going to trust?"

Family was a delicate topic for both him and Grier, and it had grown more brittle after Odette's betrayals came to light. He trusted his mother, to an extent, but his father had passed away, and he was an only child with no extended family. Grier trusted none of her blood relations. Neither did he.

But Hood was a member of the family they had chosen, and he had earned his place. They all had. It made a difference when you weren't expected to trust based on sharing DNA, as if family never lied or hurt you, but rather chose to give trust to someone who had earned it.

They reached the trapdoor, and Hood made a hand gesture to tell Linus he would open the hatch while Linus advanced on Kylie. The teen had already met him. She would be less traumatized to find him in her hidey-hole than a stranger. But when Hood leveraged the door open, and Linus shined his light down onto the pallet, it was empty.

Linus glanced up at him. "She's not here."

"Yeah," Hood said, nostrils flared. "She is."

He jumped down and began a search of the sleeping area. He was less worried about respecting her personal space than Linus had been, under the circumstances, and he located a second trapdoor when he pushed the pallet aside.

Waiting for Linus to join him, Hood assumed the same position and tugged the trapdoor open.

The space beneath was a simple square room with a mini-fridge, a microwave, and enough jugs of water to last one person a week or more. Kylie sat at a table made from an old Coke crate, her face illuminated by an electric camping lantern. An ancient formula can held plastic utensils, and she selected a fork as he watched. His presence finally registered, and she paused with a scoop of macaroni and cheese from a microwaveable cup halfway to her mouth.

With the ease of long practice, he donned his Professor Woolworth mask, his least intimidating persona. One he had designed and refined over time to put his students, just a few years older than her, at ease.

"Kylie," he soothed in the tone he reserved for spooked familiars, "you need to come with me."

Thanks to the light from her electric lantern, Linus witnessed the first tear fall. "What's happened?"

The girl's leap straight to worst-case scenarios told him she was more informed than she had let on.

"Your grandparents..." He struggled to form a proper condolence when no matter what he said, it would ruin her. "They were killed last night."

"No, no, no." She dropped her face into her hands. "This can't be happening."

In the end, there was only one thing to say. "I'm sorry."

For the second time in his life, he watched a young girl's world crumble to dust at her feet, and he mourned the loss of her innocence as he had with Grier.

"They used to let me play down here as a kid. It was my secret lair. I had no idea that they..." She rocked back and forth. "They told me to get out." She sobbed. "They told me to..."

Slowly, Linus climbed into the space with her. "Kylie, we need to move you somewhere safe."

Their new proximity allowed him to send tendrils of his magic questing toward her, but she read as human to him, making the vampires' interest in her family even more peculiar.

"I told them I would stay until after…" She hiccupped. "I can't break that promise."

"What do you know about the haunting?" Linus settled onto the floor in lotus position so that he didn't loom over the seated teen. "Tell me the truth this time."

Dust sifted down onto his shoulders from the overhead gap, and Kylie skittered against the back wall.

"Who's there?" She brought her knees to her chest. "Who's with you?"

"A friend." Linus held up his hands, including the one with the sigil. "Hood?"

Moving carefully, Hood ducked his head in and waved. "Hey, Kylie."

"W-w-what's wrong with your hands?" White shone around the edges of her eyes as comprehension punched through her grief. "They're glowing."

"Magic," Linus said simply.

"What are you?" She shrank into a ball. "You're not demons." She squinted at them. "Right?"

"We're something else." Linus saw no reason to get into the specifics. "We're the good guys."

"How do I know that?" She wet her lips. "What are you doing here? Really?"

"He really brought his new bride on a ghost-hunting excursion," Hood said without moving. "She's got a thing for haunted history, so he thought solving the mystery of this place would tickle her funny bone."

Kylie blinked a few times. "You're one freaky strange dude then."

Linus smiled, not disagreeing. "How can we convince you that you're safer with us than you are alone?"

"I'm not safe anywhere unless I do my duty." She uncoiled a bit. "I have to stay."

"Why?" Hood settled in with an open smile. "What's so important that only you can do it?"

"There's a demon in the maze." A shiver rolled through her. "It won't come up as long as I'm here."

Hood kept his tone even. "How do you figure that?"

"I'm an Oliphant." Her shoulders straightened a fraction. "It's scared of us."

Biblical demons were not creatures Linus had encountered. He didn't know anyone reliable who had interacted with them, or angels either. Creatures suspected of those designations were routinely debunked by the Society after they had been captured, killed, or brought in for examination. With Faerie leaking into this world in slow degrees, there was no shortage of the strange and miraculous, and that didn't touch on Earth's natural wonders.

Turning that over in his head, Linus asked, "The demon in the maze is separate from the shadow cats?"

"Yes." A flicker of hesitation marked her next words. "The shadow cats are guardians."

"They're aggressive toward outsiders?"

"Yeah." She ducked her head. "That story I told you about when I was a kid wasn't true." She picked at her nails. "They've got a thing about the stairs. They hang out there a lot. Once a shadow cat did trip a guest. She fell and broke her leg." She risked a glance up at him. "It sounded like the kind of thing you wanted to hear, so that's what I told you."

The dart of her eyes, the careful phrasing, made him wonder if she wasn't still attempting to read him.

"Your grandparents took care of you. They loved you." Linus regretted the fresh wash of tears down her cheeks, but he had to fill in the blanks. "Why did you lie to us about your homelife?"

"They warned me," she whispered, barely a sound. "Grams told me if..." She swallowed. "She told me if the worst happened, to take their emergency money and run." A brittle apology tipped her mouth. "When you showed up flashing Benjamins, I figured the fatter my cushion, the more comfortable I would be until I got back to Mom."

She shrugged. "She's in Oregon." Her bottom lip trembled. "She hated it here, hated her parents too." She squared her shoulders. "That's why I can't let Grams and Gramps down. I'm all they had left."

"I understand you want to honor their memories," he countered, "but why stay down here? Why not move to a room upstairs? You'll be safer there."

Barring the vampires in residence, of course.

"The maze extends five more floors below this one. The demon has never escaped its room, but I can't tell the shadow cats to stay and fight in case it does. They'll just follow me out."

That, at least, explained how the shadow cats gained access to the house from the basement.

"You're the bait," he realized, not for the demon itself but for its jailers.

"Sure." A frown gathered across her forehead. "I guess."

"This complicates things." Linus shared a lingering glance with Hood. "Any ideas?"

"Don't talk over me like I'm not here." Her voice trembled. "I'm not a dumb kid. I get a say in this."

"You're in more danger than you know," Linus warned. "We can't, in good conscience, leave you."

"You don't get a choice." She reached behind her and drew a gun she pointed at him. The weapon shook in her grip, but she switched off the safety, and her finger brushed the trigger. "I don't want to hurt you, but I'm not going anywhere until this is over."

A sigil could put her to sleep, but he would have to get close to draw it on her, and he might not survive the attempt. Better to withdraw now than risk leaving with more holes than he arrived with, which would not amuse his wife.

"All right." Linus raised his hands. "If you feel that strongly about it, we'll go."

"Thank you," she breathed, more tears falling. "I'm sorry about this."

Careful not to spook her, Linus rose and climbed up to join Hood in her sleeping area.

"Here's my card." He tossed it down to her. "Call if you change your mind."

Angling her body to keep the wobbly barrel aimed at them, she fumbled the card into her pocket.

Linus kept his hands where she could see them. "Will you answer one more question before I go?"

"It depends."

Fair enough. "Have you been to the library lately?"

"Not since I was a kid." Her confusion rang with honesty. "I read ebooks on my phone."

"Thank you," he said, and left before her fear got the better of her.

As Linus and Hood ascended to the basement, the door concealing Kylie slammed closed behind them.

"The kid's brave." Hood exhaled once the danger had passed. "I'll give her that."

"Determined too." Linus shut the door leading into the subbasement. "I have the supplies for what we'll need to extract her in my kit."

Hood took the pantry exit. "What did you have in mind?"

"I have the proper herbs for a sleep potion. It's vapor, not an ingestible. I can brew it, pour it into a thurible, and set it in the subbasement entrance. We can collect her once she's unconscious. That way no one gets hurt."

"Brewing potions is witch territory, isn't it?"

"This particular blend is one necromancers employ during voluntary resuscitations."

"No offense to you or to Grier, but I don't get it." Hood let them into the kitchen proper. "How does a person of sound mind and body decide it's prime time to get murdered and brought back as a bloodsucker?"

"Humans will do anything for more time." A smile curved his

mouth. "Even give up what they have left." He shut the basement and pantry doors behind them. "You have fae blood. You'll live ten times what the average human will or more. You'll live twice as long as Grier and me."

Old creatures had trouble weighing time. It slid through their fingers like water. Only mortals clutched at each individual drop rather than let it fall.

Hood twitched his shoulders as if discussing age made him uncomfortable. "Do we have to worry about your concoction?"

"No," Linus murmured, resting his hand on the pantry knob. Fingers drumming, he considered his options. "It only affects humans."

Gwyllgi from both Hood's and Lethe's bloodlines were half gwyllgi and half warg. Wargs were half human and half wolf, but gwyllgi were half fae and half creature. Both possessed too little human blood for it to bother them.

"You don't have to worry about locking her in," Hood said, reading him easily. "She pulled a gun on you to win a standoff, yeah, but she doesn't strike me as malicious." He washed up and dried his hands. "More like desperate. Her grandparents might have loved her, but they messed with her head too."

As his mother's sole heir, Linus recognized the Oliphants had groomed Kylie to step into their role, whether she realized it or not. And he understood the crushing weight of obligation that came with it.

But what, exactly, did their duties to the creature they believed their ancestor entombed entail?

"There must be more to it." Linus scrubbed his hands. "Her presence alone, even with the shadow cats, wouldn't deter a creature worthy of this construct. She's keeping secrets."

Before dusk, they needed answers, and there was only one place to get them.

"We need to return to the Oliphants'." Linus claimed a bottle of water from the fridge, passed it to Hood, then selected another for himself to wash the dust down his throat. "Kylie claims this is a family tradition, which means the information is getting passed down through one medium or another."

"The tapes and photos might be the extent of it. Oral traditions are common for this sort of thing."

Hunter families often took their secrets to the grave. Hood was right about that. Without knowing more about the Oliphants, it was hard to decide where they fell on the spectrum of indoctrinated humans.

"Kylie believes she's all that's standing between a demon and its escape." Linus unslung his kit from his shoulder and rested it on the counter. He flipped it open then arranged his supplies, including a resin and bone thurible hung from a silver chain. Certain he had all he required, he selected a pot to heat the ingredients. "The Oliphants, the later generations at least, might not have been indoctrinated into our world beyond their small corner if they believed that was true."

Humans accepted angels and demons without much fuss, but the shadow cats weren't common lore. In fact, he had no idea what they might be without further study. There was too much overlap in such areas to be certain from a glance. Or a scratch.

"The religious angle," Hood agreed. "Their home was decked out in Catholic paraphernalia. They might have shared the burden with their priest."

"Or they might have feared confession would get them excommunicated and kept silent."

Religion often wasn't the most forgiving institution, despite tenets espousing the contrary.

With the brew simmering, Linus turned the stove on low, covered the pot, and gestured to Hood. They returned to the cottage in silence befitting the tomb it had become for its former inhabitants.

Linus wiped off the sigil sealing the house, and the magic dissipated in a rush of stale air. This time when they opened the door, the scent of decomposition curdled Linus's stomach, and he wished he had taken a deep breath on the porch.

No matter how often he had been in the presence of violent death, he never got used its sensory horrors. He hoped he never did. No one whose duty was to stand for victims should become numb to their plight.

"The vampires had the advantage of knowing what they were searching for," he said, "but they still had no luck."

"Let's see if ours is any better," Hood sighed, his gaze drawn to the dead, and began to search.

Kylie had given them a place to start with the family-history angle. It was more than they'd had on their last visit. But it didn't explain the vampires' interest in the house, its resident haunts, or its caretakers.

From all appearances, they had killed Mr. Oliphant in a fit of temper. Linus had to believe that meant the vampires left empty-handed. But what had they wanted from these people? Had the Oliphants even known vampires existed? Or had they assumed the couple were demons come from hell?

All he knew for certain was the Rogoffs had gone through a lot of trouble to worm their way into the inn. They wanted to be present for the murderversary—tonight—but why?

Hood and Linus scoured the cottage from top to bottom, finding more than one secret cubby Mr. Oliphant hadn't given up since their contents remained neat and organized. Paperwork in a large safe hidden under the floors contained the deed to the cottage, the inn, and the enormous land parcel where both sat. There were also stacks of one-hundred-dollar bills, more than enough to fund Kylie's return to her mother.

But there was no damning evidence to explain what, exactly, the demon in the basement was or how it claimed its victims. There was no family grimoire or history or documentation to indicate how the Oliphants had become the custodians of the demon or how they learned of its existence in the first place.

"They kept no records." The lack amazed Linus. "Theirs must be a completely oral history."

"Whatever bedtime stories Kylie was hearing at night, they didn't prepare her for this." Hood flipped through another photo album then set it aside. "The poor kid is in over her head and sinking fast."

"This might explain the vampires' escalation from previous cycles." Linus identified a packet at the bottom of the pile with a realtor's logo on the front. A quick check confirmed his suspicions. "The Oliphants wanted out, or they wanted to get Kylie out." He showed Hood the signed contract dated last week. "They sold the property."

"That would definitely snatch a knot in their tails." Hood tugged on one of the sandy-blond strands that had fallen over his shoulder. "Introducing themselves to you and Grier was a gamble. Killing on the property while you're in residence? That's suicide."

"Yet they thought it was worth the risk."

"If we're right, and the Oliphants had no supernatural connections, they had no idea who you two are." His gaze drifted toward the bodies. "But there's not a necromancer or vampire alive who doesn't know Grier's name." His focus shifted. "Or yours."

The reminder gave him chills, and the void howled in his core, craving vengeance he would never taste for the harm dealt to Grier.

Lacroix and Odette had made certain before their deaths to expose her gifts to the Society. As rare as goddess-touched necromancers were, she would never fully escape the spotlight, no matter how much time passed. Thanks to that final bit of cruelty, there would always be those who coveted her, and her powers.

The truth was, as much as it pained him to admit it, Grier was no longer safe outside of Savannah, where their allies were only a phone call away. Her connection to the land, to the city itself, also protected her. This far from home, she didn't have that. As much as he wanted Grier to himself, he was grateful Cletus, Lethe, and Hood had invited themselves along.

For the most part.

"This can't be about Grier." Linus spoke out loud, as if voicing his hope made it true. "No one knew we were coming here except for the two of you, Mother, and Neely."

Woolly, Oscar, and Cletus had also known, of course, but they were above reproach and uncorruptible.

"Relax." Hood clasped his shoulder. "This has nothing to do with her."

As much as Linus wanted to believe that, as much as the evidence supported it, Grier had enemies and a knack for getting into trouble.

Done with the cottage, for good this time, Linus and Hood left, and Linus sealed it behind them.

"I need to return to the kitchen." He checked his phone. "If the pot burns, I'll have to start over, and we don't have that much time."

"How much longer does it need?"

"Two or three hours on a low simmer would be best. Then another hour or two after I set up the thurible in the basement for it to sink low enough to affect Kylie." He set out for the inn. "I need to check on Grier, then I'll get back to it."

"Stay with her." Hood kept pace with him easily. "Send Lethe down. We're both fresh. We can handle the watch." He chuckled. "My mate can't cook, but she's an old pro at stirring the pot."

Linus chuckled, but he cut it short in case this was one of those *I can poke fun at my mate, but you can't* situations. With Hood and Lethe's twisted sense of humor about matehood, he was never quite certain. "Are you sure?"

"Sure, I'm sure. I wouldn't have offered otherwise."

Hood was aware of Linus's peculiar sleeping patterns, but he was giving him an out. An excuse to watch over Grier. He almost didn't take it, but Grier was teaching him that relationships required the flex and bend of compromise in order to work. That included friendships.

"Thank you."

"No problem." He patted his stomach. "You do have food in those fridges, right?"

"I stocked up before we arrived, with Grier's appetite in mind. There's more than enough for Lethe."

"I like how you know I was thinking of my mate." Hood chuckled. "I'm lucky she's an alpha from an alpha family. Otherwise, I couldn't afford to feed her." He sobered. "And if you think about telling her I said that, or the pot comment, I will rip out your throat before you get the chance."

"Understood."

They entered the foyer, and Linus went to check on the vampires. Their room was silent, and Hood confirmed they were still in there, sleeping. Linus removed the sigil from the doorframe. With Hood on guard duty, they weren't going anywhere. If they woke to find themselves locked in, it would put them on the offensive, and he wanted to end this without further bloodshed if possible.

Hood padded into the kitchen to make sandwiches while Linus took the stairs at a clip back to Grier.

The sigil on the door erased under his thumb, and he nudged it open a crack.

Grier was curled on her side, unconscious. *Safe.* Lethe was wading through the emails and texts required to keep her pack functioning in her absence. He could tell from the doodles on her notepad.

I'm not made out of money.

Sides of beef don't grow on trees.

Moo.

$$$

The end of the month was right around the corner. She must be haggling with the butcher for their shipment of beef, pork, and chicken. Their allotments didn't last long with so many bottomless stomachs to fill.

Lethe gathered her things quietly, eased off the mattress, then winked at Linus on her way past.

After shutting the door behind her, he set a timer for three hours, drew a sigil on the doorframe, and climbed into bed.

TEN

Happily, the extra work I put in on my shredded calves while Linus fixed breakfast did the trick. I was still tender, and pulling on jeans later would suck, but I had fused the furrows together.

I was calling it a win.

With no one around to fuss at me for picking at the bandages, I removed them and confirmed the scratches had healed. The silvery lines would fade over time, and even if they didn't, I could live with them. It's not like they would get lonely. I was a patchwork of hard-earned scars that made me the tiniest bit proud. They proved I had found purpose, that I was making a difference, and if that difference was reflected on my skin...

Worth it.

Totally worth it.

Wiggling my toes, I was about to test standing when Linus let himself in, his arms laden with carbs.

"You spoil me." I made grabby hands. "I like it."

Smiling his littlest smile, the one reserved just for me, he joined me on the bed and set the tray over my lap. "We have a problem."

"Another one?" I dug into my home fries, savoring the crunchy skin on the potatoes. "Shocking."

While I shoveled food with gusto, he filled me in on how everyone else had spent their day.

"She pulled a *gun* on you?" A piece of egg fell out of my mouth. "Who does that?"

Supernatural baddies tended to attack with teeth, claws, and/or magic. Then again, we were dealing with humans. Guns were their answer to the lack of all of the above. Swords were popular too, but guns? How mundane.

Our reputations preceded us these days. Not many would tangle with one of us, let alone both of us. For two lone vampires, it would be suicide. But I had discovered during my time as potentate that factions were more than willing to band together to take me down. Or try to. With Linus and the city on my side, I was safe as houses in Savannah. It was everywhere else we had to be careful.

This should have been a fun getaway spent investigating and making out. Instead, it had snowballed into a hot mess I felt duty-bound to resolve. If not for the Oliphants' sakes, then for Kylie's. The poor kid deserved what closure we could offer.

"Bishop hit me back this afternoon." I palmed the stack of library print-offs on the nightstand I had used to write down his findings. "We must have piqued his interest." I shrugged. "That or he's bored with you gone and had nothing better to do."

"With Bishop, it's likely to be the former." Linus smiled. "Ask him, and he'll tell you he's always got something better to do."

"Are you ready for this?" I settled into storytelling mode. "It's a doozy."

Linus made himself comfortable and waited for me to begin.

"Twenty-five years ago, two darling little girls were staying at the inn with their parents. The folks wanted some alone time and sent the kids out to explore the property. The kids came skipping back with super cool sticks they found in the forest and used them to swordfight on the lawn. Except, they weren't swords. They were bones. Femurs. Two different lengths, two different patinas, which indicated two different bodies."

"Ah." Linus sat back. "More than just a head was discovered on the property then."

"Yes." I skimmed my notes. "The parents freaked and called the police. The police came out, had the girls lead them to their sword stash, and discovered a mass grave containing fifteen bodies." It got creepier from there. "They searched the surrounding area and discovered two more pits full of bones." I glanced up at him. "That would account for the missing locals."

And the severed head. It too must have been revealed by weather or time.

"There's only one reason why a sensational discovery on that scale wouldn't make it into the news." Linus frowned. "Otherwise, it would have made headlines nationwide."

"It should have," I agreed, "but it didn't."

The Society tended to live and let live when it came to humans. They wouldn't step in to spare humans from paranormal predation without incentive. Unless they stood to gain from helping, they simply didn't care.

Brutal, but that's the Society for you. No wonder Maud had despised the institution. She had enrolled me in public school, not only to keep my nature hidden, but to humanize me. She wanted me to learn empathy and knew it wouldn't come from rubbing shoulders with other High Society darlings in a prep school environment.

"The incident was contained." He shook his head. "The Society, or perhaps the Undead Coalition, called in the cleaners to erase the evidence."

"I followed up on Bishop's hunch. The cleaners' database lists the causes of death as unknown. There were no visible signs of trauma to the bones, and the oldest dated back over two hundred years. There's also no record of who reported it to the cleaners. They marked it as an anonymous tip."

"The Oliphants knew about the bones being found. The parents would have gone straight to them. Failing that, the police would have alerted them when they arrived. They would have been interviewed." His lips firmed. "Either they're more educated in our ways than we assumed, and they called the cleaners in to cover up their mess, or…"

"Our buddies the Rogoffs, who admitted to this being their favorite vacation destination every thirty years, caught wind of it and did it for them. Meaning they've got a stake—no pun intended—in all this."

Either scenario cast the Oliphants in a bad light. If the Rogoffs called in the cleaners, the Oliphants might have sighed with relief when nothing came of the bones for the simple fact their discovery would have ruined them. They might have been too grateful the incident got swept under the rug to kick up dust over it. But that still left them aware of a cache of human bones on their property and no interest in pursuing justice for whoever put them there.

"The pun was intended." His chuckle lit up his eyes. "But I agree."

"Either way, the Oliphants escaped without so much as a slap on the wrist."

"Both the severed head and the bone caches were found during or after the last cycle. That implicates several generations of the Oliphants in addition to the current one. The burden must have been too much for them. They were getting sloppy in their old age." Linus stole a slice of bacon from my plate, and I didn't even snap my teeth at him. He crunched on it thoughtfully. "Fear of another slipup this time, one that got them caught, might have spooked them into selling the place. Kylie would be left on her own if they were sent to prison."

"*If* they were responsible for the most recent kidnappings and murders, it was a lot to put on two people their age." I hated to ask, but one of us had to put it out there. "Do you think Kylie is involved?"

"She's involved," he said without hesitation. "Whether she's committed any crimes? I just don't know."

"This would all be so much easier with her cooperation."

"If it was easy, the mystery would have already been solved."

"There is that." Pushing the tray back with a sigh, I washed down breakfast with my smoothie. "Delicious as always."

I leaned over and kissed him, aware he could taste his blood and berries on my lips. That Linus accepted me and my weird biology made me love him that much more. I might have delved into exactly how much I loved certain parts of him if the door hadn't blasted open as Lethe barreled into the room.

The groan I swallowed came out as a frustrated growl and left Linus hiding a smile.

"Time to go." She tapped her watch. "Kylie ought to be sleeping like a baby."

"Wait." I glanced between them. "What?"

Linus filled me in on all I had missed while I stood and tested my balance.

"Good call." The girl had been safe enough during the day, and the fog-like potion would put her to sleep without harming her. It was the best way to extract her without anyone getting hurt. "Where's Hood?"

"Eating breakfast with the vampires." She rolled her eyes. "Barb insisted on cooking for him."

"Barb?" Shock rolled through me. "You let him eat her cooking?"

"He's not eating it." She laughed softly at my horrified expression. "He's just cutting it up and moving it around on his plate to keep them occupied until we get down there."

That was good news then. The vampires didn't suspect we were on to them if they were playing nice.

"The sun went down fifteen minutes ago." Linus gazed out the darkened window. "Their manners won't last much longer if they don't get what they came for soon."

With that in mind, I grabbed clothes fit for a rescue mission then ducked into the bathroom to dress. I left the door open so I could listen in. Plus, it's not like I had anything either of them hadn't seen.

"What real significance could the date have?" Lethe anchored her hands on her hips. "It's not like an actual portal from hell is going to open."

"Spells grow stale over time." He spoke to her but watched me wrestle with my clothes. "There's power in ritual, in anniversaries. Most spells are weakest a year and a day after they've been cast. That's when you must renew them or allow them to deteriorate."

"Why does this happen every thirty years if spells are on an annual timer?" I twisted my long hair in a high ponytail as I exited the bathroom. "Wouldn't the cycle be a yearly event?"

"Human sacrifice is the most powerful fuel for dark magic." He tugged out a dryer sheet that somehow ended up in my back pocket like a magician performing the handkerchief trick. "It might not be required as often, or smaller rituals might be performed each year on the anniversary, building toward the three-decade mark. There are too many variables and not enough information to be certain."

"You're saying whatever the vampires want is stuck in a magical cage with a lock that can only be picked once every thirty years?" Lethe cocked her head. "They've failed so far. It must be worth a *lot* to them if they're willing to brave you two to get it."

"The vampires' involvement might also explain the murders." I stomped on my sneakers, and I was ready to go. "They could have been killing anyone who saw the unexplainable or who asked the wrong questions."

A mass grave for their victims wasn't very vampiresque, though. It bordered on downright sloppy. They tended to catch and release, not murder their prey. Victims in the reported numbers begged humans to take notice, and vampires had survived as a species this long by avoiding that at all costs.

"The Rogoffs have extra incentive." Linus opened his laptop to reveal the Oliphants' email inbox, and my eyebrows climbed until he said, "They stuck their log-in information on a Post-it beside their computer."

"That logo looks familiar." Lethe leaned over his shoulder. "Are those all realty companies?"

None of the names were ones I recognized, but that wasn't saying much. I could barely list the national brands in my neck of the woods. I inherited my home, and Linus gifted me my business. Real estate had never been a concern of mine.

"The Oliphants listed their ancestral home for sale six months ago with the caveat it be sold to a developer and not as a residential property." He opened the topmost one. "There was a heated bidding war that resolved just last month. The papers were signed and notarized last week."

"That might explain why no tourists went missing this cycle." I nudged her to one side so I could see too. "What is that?" The blueprints included a mishmash of elements that didn't mesh. "Is it all one store?"

"Oh, I've seen these." Lethe pointed to the screen. "They sell guns, ammo, hunting gear, boats, ATVs." She gestured to another area. "They keep huge aquariums full of native fish." The final area she tapped. "They have restaurants too."

"That's a lot going on for one store."

"They also have candy kitchens." Her gaze went distant. "I'm talking fudge, sugared nuts, taffy."

"How have I never seen one of these?"

"You don't hunt or fish or really do the outdoors period." She shrugged. "You're an indoors girl."

"Hmm." I frowned. "I see your point."

"There are four other proposals." Linus got us back on track. "The end result in each is, as requested, the house gets knocked down and the entire property gets buried under tons of concrete and asphalt."

"No maze, no demon." I leaned against the door. "So, what's the plan?"

"We're within our rights to question the vampires about the Oliphants' deaths." Linus closed his laptop and joined me. "There won't be a jurisdictional issue, even across state lines."

Seeing as how we were both potentates, and this area lacked one, we were, in essence, the law.

The ring of Linus's cell interrupted our strategy session, and his expression when he read the caller ID spoke volumes.

"Hello?" He switched the call on speaker. "This is Linus Woolworth."

Fabric rustled, wood groaned, and the line crackled and hissed.

Eyes on mine, he thinned his lips. "Kylie?"

"There's this weird fog, and I hear something," she whispered, a dreamy quality in her voice. "Banging."

A shiver hopped, skipped, and then jumped down my spine. "From above or below?"

The kid ought to be sawing logs in Dreamland. That she had yet to fell a single tree meant she was either too stubborn to succumb, which rarely happened, like one in a thousand, or she wasn't fully human.

The thinning of his lips told me he was recalling the moment he tested her, and his findings. He believed she was human, and Linus was rarely wrong. If she possessed any magic, it was latent, buried deep within her.

"Below." She swallowed audibly. "Far below."

Lethe vibrated with tension that jittered through her voice. "Are you sure it's not your shadow cats?"

"They're silent." She hesitated. "Grier...?"

"No," she said. "Lethe. I'm Hood's—"

"—wife," I finished for her, making a cutting motion across my throat.

The kid's paranormal worldview was narrow. We didn't need to widen it more than necessary.

Linus brought the speaker closer. "What do you know about your grandparents' plans to sell the inn?"

"They told me they were too old to stand watch." Kylie stuttered, "T-t-they wanted out."

"What about your parents?" I hated to ask, but we needed to know where they fit in.

"Dad's in prison, has been since I was two. Mom moved across the country to be close enough for weekly visitation." Her breath caught. "I hated living all week for those minutes with him, so when I was old enough, I begged my grandparents to take me in. I've been living with them full-time for the past eight years."

The poor kid had been through enough. No wonder her grandparents didn't want to dump this in her lap too.

"Once the chain of succession was broken, I couldn't have accepted the position anyway." Her voice got softer. "Mom won't come back. Ever. She hates this place, and she hates—hated—her parents. Without her, only my grandparents had the power to contain the demon."

A line of succession, a magical one, threw more weight toward the Oliphants being, well, magical.

"They trained you enough to get to this point," Linus said gently. "But they never meant for you to stand guard alone, did they?"

"No," she said softly. "I thought maybe...just this one last time...I could do it. For them." She coughed, and I pictured the mist filling her lungs. "We have to be out in two weeks, and then it's over. The family curse will finally end after the house is destroyed and the basement is sealed forever."

"Can we come down?" I held a finger to my lips before the protests about waiting until she was unconscious started. "Help you figure this out?"

"Yeah." She coughed again, softer this time. "The gun isn't loaded. I found it in the kitchenette."

I didn't see the Oliphants leaving a weapon, loaded or not, where guests or their children might stumble across it, so she must mean the subbasement kitchen. Maybe that's why she had it close at hand when Linus paid her a visit.

"Sit tight." I rubbed my forehead. "We'll be right there."

"Okay," she whispered and then laughed until I worried she couldn't stop. "I'll be here."

Linus ended the call and quirked one eyebrow in reprimand, but I made a helpless gesture.

"She's a kid." I lifted my hands. "She needs our help." I let them fall. "We can't afford to wait her out."

"She pointed a gun at Linus," Lethe growled, protective instincts kicking in, which I found adorable given she was defending my husband with the same ferocity as me. "We've only got her word it's not loaded."

"You heard her on the phone," he countered. "The fog has reached her. She'll be unconscious by the time we arrive."

"Are you sure it's working?" I eyed the phone. "She's more coherent than I expected at this stage."

Given how long he had mentored me, he knew I wasn't calling his skill into question but her heritage.

"She's fighting it. Usually, they don't." He rubbed his thumb across the screen. "There could be other factors in play. We just don't know enough about the Oliphants, and we're out of time to learn."

"There's one more teeny-tiny issue," Lethe reminded us. "She heard banging."

"Demons don't exist." I flicked a glance at Linus's pensive expression. "Or, if they do, this will be the first verified sighting."

Cletus appeared in a flash of tattered cloak and moaned at Lethe, pointing a damning finger at the hall.

"Hood," she breathed and bolted down the stairs.

I was hot on her trail, my calves burning, but I was there when we spotted Hood collapsed in a heap on the floor in the dining room. I hit my knees beside him and checked his pulse. Aside from the nasty gash matting his hair in the back where he had been struck, he appeared to be in one piece.

"They called in reinforcements," Lethe growled, touching her mate's face. "That's why they were making nice with the food. They were buying time for backup to arrive."

"I got this." Using my pocketknife, I cut open my palm and drew a healing sigil on Hood. "Time to rise and shine." I pushed magic through the design, and the wound closed before our eyes. "Feeling better?"

"Ungh."

"I'll take that as a yes." Lethe helped him into an upright position. "Any idea how many?"

"Four in addition to the two, so six total." He rubbed his head. "I should have scented them."

"I shouldn't have left you alone." Lethe kissed his boo-boo. "I got worried about Grier and…"

"I know." He leaned against her. "I know."

Based on the expression Linus wore, I wasn't the only one who wished they knew what those two were talking about, but Lethe had made it plain she wasn't coughing up any answers yet, and Hood let her get away with murder. Literally.

The wraith pointed toward the pantry. I got to my feet and confirmed the door to the basement had been busted open. Now that we knew Kylie was hiding out down there, we couldn't very well lock it with a sigil as we had the first time. She would have no way out, but that meant the vampires had an easy way in.

"So much for strategy." I sighed. "Guess we default to our usual *try not to die* and hope for the best."

Before we went down, I drew sigils for light on each of our palms, and the glow was blinding.

"I've got an idea, but it might not work as well or at all on vampires' heightened senses." I drew a sigil at the base of Lethe's throat. "This will muffle our footsteps and voices." I did the same for Hood and Linus. "It won't conceal our scents, though. And it won't make us invisible. We need to stay out of their line of sight and whatever the equivalent of downwind is indoors if we want to stay off their radar."

"Will we have room to shift?" Lethe swept her light beam back and forth. "Or are we stuck on two legs?"

"There's room," Hood confirmed. "It will be tight, but that's as much in our favor as against it."

No prey in their right mind wanted to be stuck in a tunnel with two gwyllgi on the hunt.

Lethe refused to let me go first. She was an alpha, had been raised by one and groomed for the position all her life. She had trouble sitting back and letting others shield her. Even if it was only the difference of one spot in line, she was still driven to be at the head.

Hood offered an apologetic smile but climbed in after her.

Make that two spots.

Ugh.

Linus and I exchanged a glance, and I read my worry on his face. "They're acting weirder than usual."

"I've been promised all secrets will be revealed when this is over."

"Me too." I chewed on my bottom lip. "I'm glad it ends tonight. They're starting to creep me out."

Determined not to go last, I wiggled through the opening after Hood. Cletus waited for me on the other side, and he did *not* look happy. Linus's shoes touched down seconds later, and his expression hinted he agreed with the wraith.

Before we started down, he set the thurible spewing mist across the floorboards into the basement and shut the door. Kylie wasn't reacting to it fast enough, and leaving it going would only hinder our vision.

"Get us eyes on Kylie," I told Cletus. "Report back on the vampires' progress."

With an unhappy moan, he did as he was told. Eventually. After a forceful mental shove from me.

Sheesh.

What was with everyone? They were all sticking to me like glue. Even more so than usual.

I hadn't been kidnapped, taken hostage, or even slightly murdered in a good six months. I was on a roll.

Hood beat Lethe into Kylie's sleeping area after he won the

quick argument that she would recognize him but not her. The rest of us huddled around the opening, but it was obvious what he would say.

"She's not here." He pried open the next trapdoor and took a deep breath. "This one is empty too."

"The vampires?" I saw nothing to indicate they had come this way, but their senses were as keen as the gwyllgi. They wouldn't waste time tossing the place if they scented Kylie wasn't there. "You tracking them?"

"They came this way, but they didn't linger." Hood sniffed out another door, this one set into the wall behind the toppled mini-fridge. "They must have some sense of where they're going."

"Or they're following Kylie's scent," Linus added grimly. "They must have spooked her, and she ran. Her senses are muddled. She's easy prey."

The guilt thickening his voice made my gut clench. This whole situation had spun out of control the instant we stepped foot inside the library, but this was one ride we couldn't afford to get off. Not with Kylie trapped below us with vampires in pursuit.

"Do you hear them?" I listened, but only faint scuffling reached me. "Can you tell how far we have to go?"

"They're deep." Lethe cocked her head. "Two more levels? Something like that."

"Kylie never said how deep she goes. She was using the first two floors, but she might move freely between more than that." I stepped toward the opening. "We need to catch them before they find her, or whatever's bumping in the night down here."

Grim determination fueled our exploration. We ranged deeper and deeper underground, and the rotten-egg scent grew thick enough to coat the back of my throat with every swallow. We got turned around on stairs that led nowhere, tried doors that opened onto noth-ing, and almost plummeted through a disintegrating section of floor-ing. The stink was so pervasive the gwyllgi lost the trail. We were searching blindly, and it wasn't going well.

Trash littered the lower levels. Cans with peeling labels, empty water jugs, even a filthy baby bottle.

"Blood." Hood flung out his arm while he investigated a dark smudge I couldn't see well from so far back. "The kid was here, and she's hurt."

How he parsed it from the sulfuric stench impressed me when my eyes were pouring water.

"Something else was down here." Lethe flared her nostrils. "Some*one* else, maybe?"

"Oh goody." I scanned the area. "You're sure its trail starts here?"

"I can't tell," Lethe growled, clearly frustrated. "That smell is screwing with me big time."

Boom. Boom. Boom.

"What's that?" I checked with Linus. "Do you think it's what Kylie heard?"

"Perhaps." A neat frown bisected his brow. "Or the vampires might be trying their luck breaking whatever magic is holding their prize captive with physical force."

A rattle shook us, and tremors spread through my legs. "My money is on the vampires."

The rhythm was too steady, too constant, for one person to maintain. Several, however...

A shadow darted past, hitting me in the ankle and almost sending me into a face-plant. "Damn cats."

The creature gazed up at me with a solemn plea in its luminous eyes, but the persistent ache in my calves reminded me I couldn't trust them.

First Hood and then Lethe snarled, and my bestie curled her lip. "This is what hurt you?"

"Maybe not this exact one, but one like it."

When it didn't attack, I waved the gwyllgi back and addressed it. "Are you here to help or what?"

It bobbed its head and darted toward a concealed hatch it pawed at until Hood lifted the piece of wood.

"It could be leading us into a trap." Lethe hit it with all the suspicion I expected her to show a cat.

"Look at the blood trail." Hood shined his palm over a crimson handprint. "Kylie went this way."

Another tremor shook the floor, and I flung out my hand to catch myself against the wall.

"Those idiots are going to bring the whole house down." I regained my balance. "They'll kill us all."

"Not if we kill them first." Lethe bared her teeth. "Let's go solve your mystery, shall we?"

We sneaked down two more levels before my duller senses picked up the conversation ahead.

"She's the last of the Oliphants," Barb insisted. "Her blood will break the spell."

"She's not the last," Benny countered. "Her mother is still alive."

"Her mother is the next in line," a third voice confirmed. "The girl might not be enough."

"We're out of time," a fourth snarled. "This is our final chance to free him."

"There's still the child," a fifth intoned. "What other purpose must it serve?"

"Yes, what of the child?" a sixth lent weight to their argument. "Perhaps both of them together are the key?"

An uncomfortable silence lapsed while the group seemed to consider that.

Me? I was racking my brain over who else they had in there. No missing persons had been reported who fit the profile, but this cycle was all over the place thanks to the impending demolition.

"No," Barb protested. "I won't harm a child."

Call me crazy, but Kylie was a child in my book, and I didn't hear any concern for her.

"We may not have a choice," Benny soothed. "We've tried everything else."

For vampires to be huddled in the dark with a human sacrifice or two on tap, they had to want their prize in a bad way, and I felt stupid for not putting it together sooner.

The thing they were after wasn't a *what* but a *who*. That must mean the demon was actually...a vampire.

The house wasn't that old, all things considered, but if a vampire was the minotaur in this maze, then it was reaching the upper age bracket for made vampires. The odds of a clan caring that much about a single individual, even a master who had gotten trapped, were slim. But one thing they did care about, very much, were Last Seeds.

Lucky for them, Last Seeds were basically immortal and indestructible. Unlucky for us, after all this time, it would be starved, insane with bloodlust, and, possibly, just plain ol' insane.

I was spitballing here, but the pieces fit.

What didn't work for me was the thirty-year sacrifice angle. Who was kidnapping and murdering people? Not the Last Seed if it had been walled up all this time. If it was a Last Seed. Its clan? I doubted it. That kind of thing drew human interest, and these vampires had most likely been the ones cleaning up after the killers.

The shadow cat rubbed against my ankle, thoroughly giving me the willies, and blinked its eerie eyes at me. Assured of my attention, it trotted off ahead, leading the way.

I didn't like this.

Any of it.

Not a bit.

We followed the cat, which had bad idea written all over it, and it led us to the door separating us from Kylie and the vampires. This one was set into a wall, and it had been ripped off its hinges, its padlock and chain thrown across the floor. This one made of stone. We really had hit rock bottom.

An electric lantern, probably Kylie's, painted the room in shadows. There was still light enough to see an ancient pentagram inlayed into the stone. It glinted, a metal of some kind. Silver, maybe? Hard to tell. Kylie sat in the middle with her hands tied behind her back and her ankles bound in front of her.

The pungent reek of magic stained the air and made breathing difficult. This was a dark place, and I don't mean because of the lack of electricity. A heavy weight pressed on my chest, crushing my lungs, a power unlike anything I had encountered up until now.

All that was bad enough, but a second form wriggled in the farthest corner. That's where the shadow cats congregated. Their presence coaxed a tiny sob from the bundle of fabric, and its contents hit me like a ton of freaking bricks.

"A baby," I mouthed to Linus. "A *baby*."

The infant settled as the cats rocked it with their paws, but their harsh yellow eyes pleaded with me, with us.

The facts Kylie had shared about the shadow cats protecting the Oliphants were fast becoming fiction. The cats didn't give her a second glance. In fact, they made a point of avoiding her. They skirted her as far as they dared to reach the infant, and they ran interference as best they could between her and the baby, not that she could move all that much thanks to her restraints.

Lethe elbowed me and pointed to Kylie's pantlegs.

They were covered in blood.

Just like mine had been.

Just like Linus's back had been.

The shadow cats had attacked her. Savaged her. Her current predicament raised all kinds of uncomfortable questions. Like where had the baby come from? Where were its parents? Had the vampires brought it as a snack or as a sacrifice...or had Kylie?

Vampires are animated by necromantic magic, but they can't perform it. Even if someone coached them through what to do and how to do it, even if they'd had time to inset the fancy circle themselves, they had no power to activate it.

That meant it had already been put here, by people who could use it.

Swallowing the sour taste in the back of my throat, I squinted through the darkness to study the faint glitter on the back wall. I really wished I hadn't. Really, really wished.

A shelf had been mounted in clear view of anyone in the circle, and it gleamed like old bone.

In a precise row across its length sat eleven human skulls, some no larger than my palm.

Goddess be merciful.

Oblivious to our presence, the frustrated vampires banged their fists until blood ran between their knuckles, but the door before them didn't budge an inch. It was magicked shut, and if blood from Kylie wasn't doing the trick, I could guess their next move.

"Perhaps we need more blood," the third voice said right on cue.

"Perhaps we need all her blood," a fifth purred. "A life for a life."

The vampires murmured in faint agreement.

"Let." *Boom.* "Me." *Boom.* "Out."

The gathering sucked in a collective breath and exhaled a single word.

"Master."

"Screw this."

For a second, I thought I was the one with the runaway mouth, but it had been Lethe.

Magic splashed around her ankles, licked up her thighs, and pulled her under its current. She was on all fours, foam building at her mouth, in the time it took me to get the heck out of her way.

Seconds behind her transformation, Hood shook out his fur and glowered at the room full of vampires.

Snatching Linus's hand, I pricked my palm and drew an impervious sigil on him and then on me. The gwyllgi had shifted too fast for me to protect them. I had to keep my fingers crossed they could hold their own against so many vampires in such a tight space.

The sigil I used to muffle our voices and movements had sloughed off after the gwyllgi transformed. The vampires, shocked to find themselves corralled, whirled on us with hisses and snarls.

"No one else has to die." Barb stepped forward, hands spread. "We only wish to retrieve our master."

"How did your master wind up down here?" I entered the ritual space, the gwyllgi flanking me. "Everyone in this room has trouble with the truth, so you'll have to forgive me if I take your word with a grain of salt."

Spotting us, Kylie thrashed and kicked, every movement inching her toward the baby, but we had to take this slowly.

"Lucius is an old vampire." Benny forced his hands open from their fists. "He slaughtered the townspeople before he was captured, staked, and buried alive. The Oliphants' ancestors built this maze above him, thinking he was a demon from hell. They thought they were performing a public service, and maybe they were. We should have seen the signs of Lucius's mental deterioration. We should have put him to rest in our clan's tomb until he recovered his senses. We failed him."

The weight of age was evident in their faces now. Gone was any semblance of humanity.

"He's been punished enough," one of the other vampires spat. "Starved for three hundred and fifty years."

"We are not equipped to make a ruling on the fairness of his sentence," Linus said calmly. "We will contact the Society and the Undead Coalition and have representatives sent to hear your case." He eyed the wall separating us from a ravening vampire. "Until such time, your master will remain interred for the safety of the people of this town."

And in this room.

The truth was, as potentates, we could slap down a ruling on the spot. But they wouldn't like it. We handed down battlefield sentences, and most resulted in the loss of a head or a stake through the heart. There was no pause button on the streets, no time to weigh crime against action when claws were flying at your throat. We were reactive, and our judgments were final.

"That will take another thirty years," a vampire screeched. "How is that justice?"

"Your master..." Linus studied them. "He's a Last Seed?"

"Yes," another spluttered. "That shouldn't come into account."

"The spell on his tomb can only be broken tonight," Barb gritted out, fangs poking her bottom lip. "You must know what the Oliphants have planned for this place. The papers have been signed, the demolition scheduled. We will *not* leave him to suffer eternally beneath a—a—a *strip mall*."

Her tone made it hard to tell which she found more offensive—the eternal suffering or the strip mall.

"Stand aside, and let us do what we must," Benny pleaded. "He can stand trial after he's recovered."

"You precipitated Mrs. Oliphant's suicide and tortured and murdered her husband," I reminded them. "The Society will be interested to hear about your master's plight, but the rules for murdering humans and leaving their bodies to be discovered are crystal."

"Mrs. Oliphant recognized us for what we are," Benny argued. "She killed herself before we laid a finger on her. Her death is no fault of ours."

"*Before* you laid a finger on her." I hit him with the flat stare I learned from Linus, and Benny caved first. He glanced away, unable to hold my gaze. "As in, you would have laid on several had she not taken matters into her own hands."

"Mr. Oliphant knew how to break the spell, and he wouldn't tell us." Old anger simmered in his voice. "We were running out of time, and he was *glad*. I lost my temper, and for that I am sorry, but the Oliphants could have avoided all this if they had only cooperated with us."

But they had chosen death, an end to it once and for all, to spare Kylie and future Oliphants from their burden.

"We have attempted to free our master for centuries." Barb's fangs were on full display. "This is the closest we have ever gotten to him. The Oliphants' deaths unlocked the wards shielding the lower floors."

And it was clear from their seething anger that they would have punched the Oliphants' tickets sooner if they had realized it would put them closer to achieving their goal.

"That's why you took Kylie." I saw where this was headed. "You figured her death would do the rest."

"We were always careful of the humans. They never suspected us." Benny narrowed his eyes on Kylie. "They are the true monsters here. We should have slayed them long ago."

The problem with ancient vampires is they tend to get cut a lot of slack. A *lot*. This master vampire was likely to get a slap on the wrist and have his time declared served. The Society didn't care much about humans. They didn't value human life. They cared enough to keep us hidden, to protect us from them, but the reverse wasn't a priority. But there were laws in place that allowed us to punish crimes in the present, and Benny and Barb were subject to those on two counts.

"Release the girl," Hood ordered, after trading one skin for another. "The Society will want to talk to her too."

They would want an explanation for the circle, for the skulls, and for the infant for starters.

Benny glowered at us, but he did as he was asked and sliced through Kylie's bindings with a knife he borrowed from the wall. He tossed it aside when Hood's upper lip quivered, then returned to the other vampires in guarding the door leading to their master.

Kylie ripped the gag out of her mouth and flung it across the room.

"Gramps and Grams were right." Her entire body trembled. "You're demons. All of you."

Vampires, but whatever at this point.

Once she got her legs under her, she dove for the wall where Benny had selected his knife and snatched its twin. She backed into the corner, eyes wild, and clutched a wound on the inside of her wrist where they had bled her. She was putting herself between the vampires and the baby, and the cats weren't happy about it. They hissed and spat, but she weathered their claws to keep the newborn safe.

"Drop it," I yelled. "Put the knife down."

"I didn't believe them," she cried, desperate for us to understand. "I didn't want to believe them."

"You're safe." I held up my hands, palms out, and advanced on her. "We're not going to hurt you."

"But then my grandparents died." The blade shook almost free of her hand. "And I found her."

"Who?" I stopped when it hit me. "The baby." The lies she told us started to make a lot more sense. "That's why you were at the inn. That's what you were searching for."

Likely, that's why the shadow cats attacked her on the stairs, to keep her away from their ward.

"My grandparents were good people," she sobbed. "But the demon..."

The vampires growled low in their throats, but one snarl from the gwyllgi silenced them.

"Explain it to us." I kept my hands where she could see them. "What happened here?"

"M-m-mom wouldn't come home. She knew what her parents did, and she didn't want any part of it." Her eyes shone. "I didn't know. I swear. When I came here to get away from her, I didn't know." Tears leaked down her cheeks. "I loved Grams and Gramps, but when they explained the importance of the date to me last year... what it meant...what they planned to do..." Thick sobs strangled her. "They *killed* people." She glanced at the wriggling fabric. "Babies."

Her confession was the link we needed between the pits of bone and the Oliphants, but the public would never hear a word of it. The cleaners would interview her, and they would make this all go away. All those families with missing loved ones would never know what happened to them, and I hated that. It was the only way for us to continue surviving in the shadows of humanity, but necessity didn't make it right.

"I threatened to call the police if they went through with it again." She gulped down a lungful of air. "That's why they sold the house. If I hadn't done that, if I hadn't pushed them, none of this would have happened. They're dead because of me."

"You saved lives by ending this." I gentled my voice. "You were brave to stand up to them and tell them what they were doing was wrong."

The weight of her burden rounded her shoulders, and tears fell off her dipped chin.

"Why didn't you tell us the truth?" I had to keep her talking. "We could have helped you."

"No one can help me." Her gaze snagged on the tiny skulls. "I'm a monster." She swallowed hard. "My whole family are monsters." She tightened her grip on the knife. "They promised me." She wet her lips. "They promised it was over, but it was a lie. I heard the baby crying the night they killed her parents, and I started looking."

"They wanted to perform the rite one last time," I surmised when she ran out of steam. "To reinforce the spells until construction was complete."

"Yeah." She sniffled. "That's what I think, but they refused to talk about it to me."

"You did everything you could to make this right."

"I guess." She wiped her nose on her sleeve. "If I had been home that night—"

"The vampires would have tortured and killed you too."

Silence from that quarter as good as confirmed it. They might not have done it outright. She might have ended up in the same predicament she faced now—playing sacrifice—but they wouldn't have let her go. Without knowing how to break the spell, they couldn't afford to show her mercy.

"Put the knife down," I said again. "You're safe now."

The metal slid from her grip to clang against the stone floor.

Slowly I closed the distance between us and wrapped my arms around her, stroking her hair while she sobbed against my shoulder.

"They're gone," she wept over and over. "I didn't want that. I didn't want *this*."

"Shh." I rubbed her back. "Everything is going to be okay."

While I held Kylie together, Hood rushed in and gathered the drowsy baby against his chest.

A moment later, he shot me a thumbs-up to let me know she was okay, and Kylie noticed.

"I found her in a crate two floors up," she rasped. "I couldn't access that level until...until..."

Her grandparents died.

They must have warded it to keep their tiny victim safe...and quiet. No wonder we hadn't heard its cries during our visits to the subbasements. The poor thing must have been starving by the time Kylie found her.

A blur smudged the edge of my vision, and a crisp snap filled my ears.

Lethe stood over the body of a vampire, its neck broken, and glared at the rest. "Anyone else?"

The knife Benny had discarded balanced on the dead vampire's open palm. She must have been making a play for Kylie when Lethe intervened. Vampire versus gwyllgi never ended well. For the vampire.

"I might be able to release your master," Linus said, eyes on the pentagram. "This is witch work, so it will be resistant to necromancy."

Benny and Barb sucked in whistling breaths, their hands finding one another and clasping.

"I'm willing to try," Linus continued, "given the timetable, but he will remain contained within a circle of my making until the Elite arrive to carry him to a secure facility. He'll require blood, a lot of it, and counselling if he's to reintegrate into the modern world."

"The clan will see to his dietary needs and his reeducation," Barb promised. "We are happy to take custody of him as soon as the Society has finished their evaluation."

"You'll also be held accountable for the library incident," I bluffed to watch their reaction. "Your clan will be expected to make an anonymous donation sufficient to fund construction of a new building."

That, along with my donation, ought to give them the funds to purchase new stock to fill all those lonely shelves.

"About that..." Benny cleared his throat. "We didn't mean for either of you to get hurt."

"You wedged a backhoe against the only exit and tried to set the trailer on fire," I said slowly. "How did you see that ending for us?"

"We only wanted you to take the hint and leave," Barb added. "We hoped it would scare you away."

Scary was knowing my mother-in-law would be deciding their fates. She wasn't big into leniency where her son was concerned. As someone intimately acquainted with her favorite pit in which to throw those she wanted forgotten, I almost pitied them.

A clan's devotion to their master could reach near fanatical heights. I had seen it before, a time or two. But their master might have been saved—along with countless other lives—had they informed the Society or the Undead Coalition of their plight right from the start.

All I could figure was the Rogoffs worried the punishment for their master's crimes would be continued entombment below the inn and decided it was too risky bringing in outsiders who might take issue with the reign of terror that landed him there in the first place.

Last Seed or not, survival of our species ranked higher than any one life in the Society's book.

"I'll get Kylie upstairs and locked down until the Elite arrive." Lethe eased the girl away from me and settled her arm around Kylie's shoulders. "We'll get a medic inbound too." The numbing agent must be at work on Kylie. She hadn't complained once about her wounds, but the blood loss was making her tipsy. That, more than the fog, had thrown her for a loop. "Hood?"

"We're coming." He booped the baby on its tiny nose. "Aren't we, cutie-pie?"

Glancing back at me, Lethe chewed on her bottom lip, but Hood nudged her through the opening.

The Society would evaluate the baby for any lasting effects of its ordeal before turning it over to human social services until any living relatives could be located. I just hoped there were grandparents out there who would step forward and give her a loving home, a second chance at happiness, like Maud had given me.

The shadow cats, every single one, followed in his footsteps and exited the chamber.

Once the gwyllgi cleared out, we still had five vampires with separation anxiety to handle.

"The price of my help is your cooperation," Linus warned Benny and Barb. "Harm one of us, any of us, and your master will never see the light of the moon again. Be it in his tomb here or in a Society prison."

"We accept your offer." Benny took her hand, and they stepped forward. "You have our word."

"They killed Sandra," one of others snarled. "You can't mean to let them get away with—"

"Our master's life is more important than hers, yours, or mine." Barb kept her tone level. "You will obey me in this, or you will take the master's place once he is freed."

The color washed out of the vampire's face, and he fell in line with the others.

"Our clan will wait for news in the dining room." Hope and resolve colored her expression when she locked gazes with her mate. "The Elite can collect us there."

Hand in hand, Benny and Barb led the others out past the body of their fallen clansman.

"Cletus." I waited for the wraith to arrive. "Give Lethe a heads-up so she can intercept the vampires."

A low moan filled the air as he rose through the floorboards overhead to play messenger.

Alone with Linus, I rubbed my forehead. "That was not at all how I pictured this going down."

Instead of saving a human from vampire predation, we were saving a master vampire from entombment by humans. Well, not humans. "Do you think Kylie knows she's descended from witches?"

"It's hard to say, given her belief in demons and ignorance of vampires." He studied the door causing all the fuss. "Her grandmother must have been the Oliphant by birth. She killed herself to keep them from using her blood to break the spell holding the master vampire captive." He mapped it with his fingertips. "Her grandmother might have relied on rituals she was taught as a child without questioning their roots." He stood back. "Given the religious paraphernalia, it's possible the family believed themselves chosen by God to do his work."

"How do they figure trapping one demon is worth all those lives?" Chills rose down my arms. "Kylie never said how the parents died, but it's clear babies and small children were the sacrifice of choice."

"Chandler Oliphant must have been the coven leader at the time of Lucius's killing spree. Assuming he was the one who cast the original containment spell, he gave his descendants a loophole to cut down on how many sacrifices were required to maintain it by allowing them to tie the ritual to the anniversary of his death."

The sickness churning in my gut only grew worse. "Did they have to use a freaking baby?"

"We lose our innocence quickly," Linus said softly, abandoning his work to come hold me. "A newborn is a miracle, a wonder." He exhaled, his breath cool along my cheek. "That's why they're targeted for spells such as these. They're wholly good and wholly innocent and full of unlimited potential."

"There's not much time left." I pushed him back gently, ready to get out of here. "Let me help?"

"I was hoping you'd offer." A smile pulled at his lips. "You break the spell, and I'll set the containment circle."

"Oh sure." I snorted. "Give me the easy job."

As it turned out, Kylie was right about the line of succession being broken. The few drops of her blood I scraped off the floor proved it. The vampires could have killed her, drained every drop onto that pentagram, and it wouldn't have made a bit of difference. Mrs. Oliphant had been the key, and she had made certain they couldn't wield her to unlock their master's cage.

Between the two of us, we managed to free the master vampire and contain him before he ripped out either (or both) our throats. Cletus hovered like a fly, buzzing around my head the entire time. He was all too eager to escort me up and out of the basement when the time came.

Standing in the empty kitchen, I dialed the cleaners' hotline while I waited on Linus to join me. I gave the operator a quick rundown of the situation, my name, and the addresses of the cottage and the inn.

The Grande Dame might be my mother-in-law, but that didn't mean I wanted to be the one who explained this on record for the Society. Linus could handle that call, and someone at the Lyceum would get in touch with the Undead Coalition on the Rogoffs' behalf.

"I located the Oliphants' grimoire." Linus exited the pantry with a leather-bound book open across his palms. "There was a cache beneath the center of the pentagram, but it hadn't been opened in decades."

Though I could guess the answer, I asked him anyway. "Find anything interesting?"

"Verification the Oliphants are descended from witches, though it appears the family was no longer practicing beyond this specific rite." He skimmed a page with his fingertip. "There's an account of the master vampire slaughtering the townspeople, just as the Rogoffs said, though Lucius is referred to as a demon throughout." He flipped a page. "Lucius, Lucifer. They thought he was the devil incarnate."

Hard to pity a vamp who got punished for getting caught with his hand in the killing spree cookie jar, but eternity was a *long* time to starve in the dark. The Society would have its hands full with this case.

"There's also a complete set of blueprints for the maze. There are other sealed doors, according to this. They were added later, over a span of years, so they're not part of the original working." He made a thoughtful noise in the back of his throat. "It appears, rather than a gateway to hell, Chandler believed the house straddled a ley line. However, his coven was unable to tap into its power. With the structure already built, they turned to sacrifice to achieve their goals."

It sounded like this was a case of having just enough magic and know-how to be dangerous.

"Are you saying there might be other missing vampires locked away?"

"The evidence indicates the Oliphant coven hunted vampires who trespassed on their territory."

"Religious zeal?"

"Fear." He tilted the book forward to show her an illustration of a witch burning at the stake. "They took care of problems before humans got wind of them in order to protect themselves." He flipped to a section near the back. "Look familiar?"

Black ink swarmed the page, but distinct eyes had been drawn in the writhing mass.

"Shadow cats." I leaned closer. "Does it explain them?"

"Yes and no." He closed the book, set it on the counter, then washed his hands. "With a major sacrifice such as the deaths of the infants anchoring so much magic in the house, the Oliphants weren't required to perform rituals on that scale to tap into the existing power structure."

"They made smaller sacrifices to cast smaller containment spells to hold less powerful vampires." A pang swept through me. "Cats."

"Black cats," he agreed. "Familiars."

"That's why their blood worked." All those poor kitties. The Oliphants must have bred them to have a ready supply on hand. "Familiars are magical conduits."

"Their souls were trapped here just as surely as the master vampire."

Uninterested in touching the book, I edged closer to him. "Breaking the spell freed them?"

"We'll know for certain at dusk." He dried his hands. "But I believe so, yes."

"Why attack guests?" I leaned my hip against the counter. "They protected the baby."

"Perhaps they hoped to scare off any potential victims, or maybe they wanted to get your attention." A shrug rolled through his shoulders. "Attacking you guaranteed we would investigate the phenomenon."

"Maybe." Or maybe they were bloodthirsty jerks who were only sympathetic to fellow sacrifices.

Linus took me by the hand and led me into the foyer. Shadows still crouched in the staircase's corners where moonlight filtered through the windows, but the darkness wasn't alive as it had been.

The cats were gone.

Bloodthirsty jerks or not, I hoped this meant they were finally at peace.

"I don't know about you." I limped up the stairs. "But I might need a vacation from our honeymoon."

His soft laughter trailed us into our room, where we showered off the dirt and horrors in anticipation of the arrival of the cleaners, the Elite, and whatever emissaries the Society and the Undead Coalition dispatched to resolve this mess centuries in the making.

ELEVEN

Noon found me sluggish and yawning. I hated staying up so late, but I didn't want to spend another day in this place if I could help it.

The foul smells had vanished along with the shadow cats, but the prickling waves of magic caressed me from time to time, and I wanted to scrub my skin raw to be rid of them. They were remnants, echoes of the dark magic containing the master vampire, and the cleaners had called in a specialized coven to deal with its removal.

Exhaustion sank its claws in me, but I didn't dare shut my eyes.

All those tiny skulls. All in a neat row. I would never forget the sight for as long as I lived.

Linus, noticing how I drooped, delivered a plate with crisp celery stalks smothered in peanut butter and topped with raisins. I hadn't eaten ants on a log since I was a kid, but I shoveled them in until I couldn't move. Or maybe until he ran out of celery. One of those two things.

Around two in the afternoon, the Elite left with Benny, Barb, and the newly freed Lucius Roque in tow. Kylie got her own escort to a different facility. There would be questions. A lot of them. And she was the only Oliphant left to answer.

Around three, the sentinels' interviews with the clan wrapped up, and the other vampires bedded down until dusk, eager to leave at nightfall and begin preparations for their master's eventual return to their clan home.

Around four, the cleaners left the cottage with the Oliphants' remains and went on standby until they got their turn at the inn.

Around five, a containment unit comprised of fresh Elite sentinels arrived to begin searching each floor of the subbasement for any survivors. They were already dead, well, undead, but Barb was right. No one deserved to be walled up for all eternity beneath a strip mall.

By the time dusk fell, I could barely hold my eyes open, and I had no idea what was going on anymore. Too many people had been in and out, too many questions had been asked, and too much time had passed since I demolished my snack.

I wanted to eat, and I wanted to snuggle Linus until I forgot what I had seen. More than that, I wanted to go home.

"You look beat." Lethe tossed me a strip of jerky, the last inch of it anyway. "Ready to go?"

"Been ready." I yawned. "I want to eat this, but I'm too lazy to make chewing motions."

"That's really sad. How about this?" She dipped into her pocket and pulled out a chocolate bar. "It will melt on your tongue, and it has caffeine. *Mm.* Caffeine."

"Chocolate and caffeine. Two of my favorite food groups." I made grabby hands at her. "Yes, please."

Hood breezed in, keys dangling from his fingers. Lethe lunged for them, and he held them high over his head so she couldn't reach, even on tiptoe.

"I enlisted a sentinel to drop our rental off at the airport," Hood told Lethe, ignoring her short bunny hops with a grin. Eyebrows raised, he checked with me. "I figured I could drive us all home in yours since Lethe would ride your bumper the whole way otherwise."

"That works for me." I checked with Linus, and he nodded. "Thanks."

Hood caught Lethe around the waist and planted a kiss on her lips, which was cute until she hooked her legs around his waist, climbing his torso like a tree to snatch at the keys.

"Lethe." He stared at her with his eyes soft but his mouth firm. "Stop putting it off. You promised."

Lethe huffed out an exhale and unclimbed her mate. "We need to talk before we leave."

In all the insanity, I had forgotten her bargain. I guess the honeymoon really was over.

"Walk with me." She linked her arm through mine then did the same with Linus. "Both of you."

We exited the inn, Hood behind us, and Lethe tugged us to a quiet spot.

"There's a very good reason why Hood and I were already on our way to you when Cletus dropped in with the perfect excuse for us to intrude," she confessed. "I didn't put it together until after you two left the wedding reception, or I would have mentioned it sooner."

Wary of her tone, I frowned over at her. "Put what together?"

"You threw up the morning after the wedding," she reminded me. "I was there, remember?"

Just recapping the wonders of the dessert table while I packed had sent me running to hug the toilet.

"We ate like fifty-billion cakes." I laughed, relieved that was her damning clue. "I was sugared out."

"That's never stopped you before," she countered. "We've eaten more and still gone back for tenths or elevenths or whatever."

"I haven't barfed once since." I crossed my finger over my heart. "What's that got to do with—?"

Linus fell behind, and his arm slid from Lethe's. His knees kind of...locked, and he stood there frozen.

"Linus?" I rushed to him and smoothed my hands down his chest. "Are you okay?"

His mouth moved, but nothing came out. His eyes were wide, startled, *panicked*.

A tremor worked from his ankles up his legs and throughout the rest of his body.

"I'll fix this." I reached for my pocketknife. "Stay with me."

Lethe put a hand on my shoulder. "Grier…"

"Speak to me." I touched the blade to my palm. *"Linus."*

Slowly, he wet his lips. "You're pregnant."

The knife tumbled from my hand to thump in the dirt. "What?"

"You're…pregnant."

Laughter burst out of me, and I doubled over, wheezing through it. "Good one."

"He's not wrong." Lethe retreated behind Hood. "I can smell it, loud and clear."

Since I was already bent in half, I didn't have a long way down to land on my butt. It still hurt, but my tailbone was used to the abuse. "I use a contraceptive sigil."

Peering around him, she reminded me, "Magic doesn't always work right on you."

"I'm on birth control."

"The pill is notoriously unreliable when taken by magical creatures."

"That's why I doubled up," I growled. "I should have been safe."

From behind Hood's back, she told Linus, "Maybe next time also wear a condom or three?"

That was all it took to tip him over. His legs gave, and he fell. He landed in a seated position, but the way he was swaying, I wasn't certain how long he would stay vertical.

"Are you…" Linus managed a whisper in my direction, "…unhappy?"

"I'm shocked." I would have crawled to him, but I couldn't feel my legs. "This was not the plan."

We had budgeted a good century of our lives for the pursuit of selfish pleasures. We were so young. We had all the time in the world, or nearly, to have kids. But all that planning evaporated with two little words.

"I'm...pregnant." I spread a palm across my abdomen. "Wait." I dropped it again just as fast. "How accurate are gwyllgi noses when it comes to these things?"

"Ninety percent or so," Hood answered for her. "The change in your hormones triggered Lethe's protective instincts. When you left for your honeymoon, she came unglued."

"It starts with the alpha and works its way down," Lethe confessed. "Before the nine months are up, every member of the pack has baby fever and can't go a day without seeing the mother-to-be."

"Oh, goddess." I clutched my head. "Linus?"

"Yes," he rasped, hunched over like the bones had been ripped from his spine.

"Are you..." I swallowed hard, "...unhappy?"

"I'm terrified." He walked over to me on his knees and gathered me in his arms. "I had hoped we would have time to determine how our gifts would mix before taking this step but..."

Peeking up at his face, which had gone paler than usual, I curled against him. "But?"

"A child," he breathed. "With you." He cupped my face in his palms. "How could that ever make me unhappy?" He kissed my forehead, my eyelids, my nose, my chin. "Woolly is going to be a grandmother."

And Cletus a grandwraith.

Tears welled in my eyes, and I let them fall. "She'll be thrilled."

His face a neutral mask, he pulled back to see me better. "But are you?"

"I'm coming around to the idea." I laughed, and we all ignored the hysterical lilt at the end. "A baby."

"A baby," he echoed. "*Our* baby."

"Are you two done panicking," Lethe asked, "or should we call an ambulance to drive you home?"

Linus and I helped each other to our feet. Then Hood and Lethe were there to embrace us.

Lethe squeezed me gently. "Congratulations, Mom."

"Thanks, Auntie Lethe."

"Buckle up," Hood told Linus as they clasped hands. "Fatherhood is a wild ride."

Too dazed to respond, Linus pumped his arm, his fingers gone limp.

Once the hugs and backslapping ended, the four of us—no, the *five* of us—headed for the rental car.

Linus and I didn't speak the whole way back to Woolworth House. We held each other in the backseat and let the gwyllgi fill the silence. There was so much to wrap our heads around and so little time to do it.

Nine months.

They would pass in a blink.

How would I patrol? How would I keep my city safe? How would I protect my child from my enemies?

The answer came to me in a rush of warmth that curled around my heart the same as I curled around my husband.

Together.

Linus and I would do this together. With a little help from our friends.

ABOUT THE AUTHOR

USA Today best-selling author Hailey Edwards writes about questionable applications of otherwise perfectly good magic, the transformative power of love, the family you choose for yourself, and blowing stuff up. Not necessarily all at once. That could get messy.

www.HaileyEdwards.net

Black Dog Series Novellas

Stone-Cold Fox

Gemini Series

Dead in the Water #1

Head Above Water #2

Hell or High Water #3

Gemini Series Novellas

Fish Out of Water

Lorimar Pack Series

Promise the Moon #1

Wolf at the Door #2

Over the Moon #3

Araneae Nation

A Heart of Ice #.5

A Hint of Frost #1

A Feast of Souls #2

A Cast of Shadows #2.5

A Time of Dying #3

A Kiss of Venom #3.5

A Breath of Winter #4

A Veil of Secrets #5

Daughters of Askara

Everlong #1

Evermine #2

Eversworn #3

Wicked Kin

Soul Weaver #1